BAD BEHAVIOR

BAD BOYS OF THE BAYOU

ERIN NICHOLAS

ISBN: 978-1-952280-49-8
Cover Design: Najla Qamber, Qamber Designs

AUTHOR'S NOTE

I've been published for over a decade and have written a lot of books in that time. I actually don't know how many. I've counted a few times before but there are short stories and novellas, bonus material, things that have gone out of print, or been re-worked… and I don't know how to count all of that. I usually say, "over fifty books" and figure that's safe.

But in all of that vagueness there are a few things that have become what I call my "orphans" over the years. Books and stories that don't really *belong* anywhere specific anymore. I was first published with Samhain Publishing which has since closed its doors, and all of those books came back to me, including stand-alone stories that didn't connect with anything else. I've also had some really amazing opportunities to participate in various projects and events and series for which I've written a story (or stories) and I've enjoyed them all! But projects end, and opportunities shift. So, over the years, projects, series, and publishers have come and gone. But the stories are still alive and well. They just don't really *fit* anywhere.

So I finally decided that I needed to give them a home. And a new chance to meet readers! They needed a new place to live. But I needed to put them all together and give them a connection to one another since they didn't have other connections.

And, where else would I make this new home than Louisiana?

Now I couldn't just bring these people (some of whom I've known since before I was published!) to Autre, the home of my other Louisiana books. They don't quite fit there. They have a different vibe. They came from a little different Erin Nicholas. Not totally different, of course. My voice and style have always been pretty consistent.

But these stories are a little grittier. More emotional. The people have a little more baggage than the Boys (and girls) of the Bayou or the people of Boys of the Bayou Gone Wild. They're also a little dirtier. There's always open-door sex scenes in my books, but in Bad, Louisiana, there are just more of them. These books just have a little different feel. And they needed their own home. Their own place to live and be what they are rather than trying to fit into something else.

So, I present to you Bad, Louisiana. A collection of books that have existed in Erin Nicholas world for a long time but have been rewritten and edited to fit together in a new town, with some new friends, for a second chance to meet readers and bring even more love stories to the Louisiana bayou!

I hope you enjoy them as much as I did when I first wrote them and loved them again going back for this reimagining.

If you're a long-time reader and are "afraid" that you might have read these books before, you can check out the original titles and more information here: https://bit.ly/BadBoys-ThenNow

WELCOME TO BAD, LOUISIANA!

These boys are only called "bad" because of their hometown…

Yeah, right.

I've been to Bad several times over the years and it always makes me smile. The town itself has an interesting history. It was originally, and very briefly, settled by a bunch of Germans. Did you know that Germans use "bad" in town names to denote a spa town? Yep, that's a thing.

So, I guess in this case, there was a small hot spring outside of town and the settlers claimed that made it a spa town in the new frontier. They named the town Bad Salzuflen and they'd hoped it would attract even more settlers. Particularly of the young and female persuasion.

But, unfortunately, the 'hot spring' was actually just a particularly marshy area (no one knows why it was so much warmer… or at least they're not saying) and then, before they could figure out what to do about that, the French showed up and ran the Germans out.

Well, after that no one could pronounce or spell Bad Salzuflen, but they didn't really want to go to the trouble of renaming the whole thing, so they just dropped the Salzuflen, painted over that part of the welcome sign, and the town decided to lean into the whole *Bad* thing. Especially in more modern times.

Seriously. The hair salon is called *Bad Hair Day?* (yes with a question mark so that when they answer the phone it's, "Bad hair day?" and you say, "Yes", and they say, "Come on down and let us fix it!" And there's so much more.

Here's a quick list:
Bad Habit—coffeeshop
Bad Brakes—auto mechanic shop
Bad Brews—bar and restaurant
The Bad Egg—diner/ cafe
Bad Gas—gas station and convenience store
Bad Faith Community Church—local church
Bad Hair Day?—hair salon
The Bad Place—the physical therapy clinic
Bad Medicine—the medical clinic
Bad Memories—community center

Instead of fighting it and letting everyone else mock them, the citizens decided to have some fun with it. And hey, they sell a lot of merch (like *I got Bad Gas on my roadtrip* travel mugs and *I've been to The Bad Place and survived* t-shirts) and no one ever forgets a trip to Bad!

So come on in and have some fun! It really will be a *good* time!

THE SERIES

You can read the Bad Boys of the Bayou in any order!

The Best Bad Boy: (Jase and Priscilla)
A bad boy-good girl, small town romance

Bad Medicine: (Brooke and Nick)
A hot boss, medical, small town romance

Bad Influence: (Marc and Sabrina)
An enemies to lovers, road trip/stuck together, small town
romance

Bad Taste in Men: (Luke and Bailey)
A friends to lovers, gettin'-her-groove back, small town romance

Not Such a Bad Guy: (Regan and Christopher)
A one-night-stand, mistaken identity, small town romance

Return of the Bad Boy: (Jackson and Annabelle)
A bad boy-good girl, fake relationship, small town romance

Bad Behavior: (Carter and Lacey)
A bad boy-good girl, second chance small town romance

Got It Bad: (Nolan and Randi)
A nerd-tomboy, opposites attract, small town romance

BAD BEHAVIOR

If you like bad boys who are good men, determined women who fight for what they want, lots of dirty talk, and quirky weird small towns… this one's for you!

Carter Shaw isn't a man anyone would mistake for a nice guy. He's has always been intense, up for anything and fearless—on the football field, when wearing his badge, and in the bedroom.

But pleasure is never confused with love. His unstable upbringing was more than enough to scare him off commitments for good.

Until he meets Lacey Andrews.

A true do-gooder, heart and soul, Lacey is the only woman to ever make Carter wish he was a better man.

It's probably a good thing his friend and partner fell in love with her first.

Even when Garrett dies in the line of duty, Carter knows he can't give Lacey everything she wants and needs. Until she shows up on his doorstep in nothing but a trench coat and blue lingerie. Now there may be a few things he can offer...

Losing Garrett has only proven how short life is and Lacey doesn't want to miss another moment of happiness. Carter is her best friend and she knows he's the only one who can make her feel alive again. But she wants to be a part of more than his bedroom. And as stubborn as Carter is, he clearly hasn't met a woman who's madly in love before.
Until now.

CHAPTER ONE

HE WOULD REALLY PREFER to be stabbed.

Not fatally, of course, but a big ol' knife in the thigh would be preferable to this.

Carter Shaw tipped back his soda, wished for something much stronger, and watched the couples dancing to some new sappy love song.

Lisa, his most recent Saturday night diversion, caught his eye and gave him a huge smile.

Christ, she wasn't even here with *him*. That Saturday night had been four weeks ago and when she'd asked him to be her plus-one tonight, he'd told her he couldn't because he was on call. Which was true. He had agreed to be on call tonight for anything that came up for the police department—so that he had an excuse to not be anyone's plus-one for the wedding.

She was dancing with another man, but still eye fucking Carter.

Which confirmed that a root canal, too, would be preferable to attending a wedding reception.

It wasn't that he wasn't happy for the couple. He was, he supposed. Whatever. They were adults and could do what they wanted.

But weddings made him itchy and wedding dances were hell.

Everyone had love on the brain, especially the single women. Everything from the pretty dresses, to the flowers, to the cake made them yearn. And made them look at the single men in the room as potential soul mates.

Put a girl in a dress in the local bar, even with cake nearby, and she just wanted to dance and make out.

Put her in a reception hall with candles and white tablecloths and a friend in a white frilly dress, and she started wanting unrealistic things. Like a guy who wasn't an asshole sometimes.

He blamed the vows.

The lovey-dovey words about forever and cherishing one another and being there through it all that made women a little nuts.

The champagne didn't help.

Deep down, the women *knew* that was asking a lot. They all knew at least three couples who had promised those same things and had been divorced and hating each other a few years later.

So what the hell happened when a woman watched a friend put on a white dress and veil? Their common sense just vanished?

The whole thing had made no sense to Carter's dad either. After four wives and countless girlfriends, Matthew Shaw was now happily fucking women twenty years his junior and making the same old bullshit promises.

And the women kept coming anyway.

If there wasn't a lesson in that, Carter didn't know anything.

He finished his Coke and straightened away from the bar he'd been leaning on.

"You're not leaving yet."

Dammit. Carter sighed and turned to see his buddy Jackson Brady grinning at him.

"Told you before, you're not my type. Where's your girlfriend?" Carter asked.

Even Jackson, one of the biggest players Carter had ever met, was wrapped around a pretty pinky finger. Carter was one of the few holdouts from their group.

"She's in the ladies room." Jackson signaled the bartender for a beer. "So seriously not even dancing huh?" Jackson asked after he'd taken a swig.

"Women at weddings have unrealistic expectations," Carter told him.

"Don't most guys look at women at weddings as easy marks?" Jackson leaned an elbow on the bar.

"Yep," Carter agreed.

"But *you* don't want to get laid tonight?"

"Not worth it." Carter contemplated getting another drink. If Jackson was going to be chatty, he might need something more. Then again, he couldn't spike it with anything, so what was the point? Whiskey was the only way his buddy's newfound wisdom and happiness about being in a committed relationship was going to be palatable.

"Jesus, Carter," Jackson said with a chuckle. "Most of the women here know you. None of *them* expect a ring. Just don't go for any new girls."

It still wasn't worth it. Most of the women here did know him and had all of his life. Growing up in a small town had its advantages. And its disadvantages. One of those being that by the time a guy got to twenty-eight years old, he'd dated and dumped most of the women he might possibly be interested in.

It wasn't like he was notching his bedpost. It was just how it was. Carter didn't do long-term. But he really liked women. What came with that naturally was a lot of exes.

"Repeats are a terrible idea at weddings," he told Jackson. "If you date a girl and break up with her and then hit on her at a wedding, she's going to think you want to start things up again."

"You've repeated with more than one woman in this room."

Carter nodded. "But I've never flirted with them at a wedding."

"That makes a difference?" Jackson was clearly enjoying this. He was grinning and drinking as if he knew that Carter couldn't drink and really wanted to.

"Of course it does. They've just watched some guy agree to love, honor and cherish one of their friends forever. They're all worked up into a romantic lather."

Jackson tipped his bottle back again. "Well, buddy, I can tell you from personal experience that when you find that one woman—"

"Spare me," Carter broke in.

Worse than watching his friends be all romantic and sweet was listening to them *talk* about it. Jackson was the worst. He was so in love with Annabelle that Carter had needed to tell him to shut the fuck up about it more than once. And Carter even really liked Annabelle and was genuinely happy for them. It was still annoying as hell.

He'd listened to and watched his father fall madly in love too.

A dozen times or more.

Four of those had even resulted in a reception hall with candles and white tablecloths and a beautiful woman in white.

The longest one had lasted four years.

Of course, the last thing Jackson had ever done was spare Carter.

"You're telling me," Jackson said, "that you have *never*, not once, not even for a little bit of time, felt like you could maybe, possibly, wake up next to the same woman for the rest of your life?"

Carter wasn't quick enough with his answer. He should have said *no* firmly with his mean-cop look. Not that his mean-cop look worked on Jackson. Jackson Brady didn't shut his mouth easily. Not even for cops. Hell, Carter had been right next to him when Jackson had mouthed off to the cops. Before Carter had his own badge, of course.

"There is someone!" Jackson crowed. "I knew it. I knew you couldn't be that closed off."

Closed off? Christ.

"It doesn't matter," Carter told him. That was for sure. "I thought maybe, possibly, *once*. But never again."

"Who was it?"

Carter shook his head. "No fucking way." He hadn't told *anyone* Lacey's name. No one on the planet knew how he felt about her—how he *had* felt about her.

He felt a punch to the gut with the thought.

Actually there was one guy who knew—who had known. His buddy Garrett. Garrett had known how Carter felt about Lacey.

But Garrett was dead now. So his secret was safe.

Jesus, even thinking that sounded weird. Garrett had been his friend. His buddy through the police academy. His work partner for the five years Carter had lived in Baton Rouge before coming home to Bad, Louisiana. And he'd been Lacey's boyfriend and then fiancé.

And he was now dead, and Carter was so fucking conflicted about his feelings about…everything. Whiskey was the only answer when it all came to mind.

And he couldn't drink whiskey tonight.

So he had to stop thinking and talking about all of it.

"No one from here," Jackson mused. "I would have been able to tell."

Carter rolled his eyes. "Whatever." No one read him. No one knew anything Carter didn't want them to know.

"Would have been able to tell what?"

Annabelle came up next to Jackson and wrapped her arm around his waist. Jackson pulled her snugly against his side.

For just a flash, Carter thought *damn, that would be nice to have.* Not with Annabelle, of course, but with…

He cut that thought off before it could fully form.

But there was one woman and there had been one chance…

"If Carter was crazy about anyone here in Bad, I would have been able to tell," Jackson told Annabelle.

Annabelle gave Carter a surprised look. "You're crazy about someone?"

"No."

"He was," Jackson clarified. "Says it over."

"It *is* over," Carter said. "It…got complicated."

That had to be the biggest fucking understatement of his life.

And the thing was, it could have been simple. All he would have had to do was say yes…to everything he wanted.

Fuck.

Fucking weddings. They even made *him* get all soft and nostalgic.

His phone rang and Carter almost cheered. He grinned as he pulled it from his pocket. Jackson rolled his eyes.

"Shaw."

"Hey, Carter, there's been a break-in," Linda, the night dispatcher, told him.

They weren't very formal in Bad. There was no need really.

"A break-in?" he repeated. That was…unusual.

Which was confirmed when Jackson snorted. "Yeah, sure."

"Yeah. Bridgett and Ken Logan's place," Linda said.

Carter was only about five minutes away. "Are they alright?" he asked, already on his way to his truck. He didn't even care where Lance, the officer on duty tonight, was. This was his chance to get out of the reception and it promised more excitement than he'd had on the job in months.

"Wait! Seriously? I'm supposed to believe there was a break-in?" Jackson called after him. "Come on, man!"

Carter shot him a scowl, but it was too late. Several people in the immediate vicinity had overheard. Dammit.

He covered the mouthpiece and called out, "Nothing to worry about! Everything is under control!"

That didn't mean there wouldn't be some curious souls who decided to head down to Maple Street. Because this promised more excitement than *any* of them had had in months.

He wound his way through the crowd toward the entrance to the community center, Bad Memories. Jase Hawkins had just recently finished remodeling the old strip club, The Pork and Peach, and it was now *the* place to hold big parties and events.

Like all the businesses in Bad, Louisiana, Jase had opted for a tongue-in-cheek name with 'bad' in it. Bad Memories joined Bad Brews, Marc Sterling's bar, Bad Gas, the convenience store and gas station, Luke Hamilton's auto shop, Bad Brakes, along with many others.

Jase hadn't yet paved the huge field to the east that would eventually be the parking lot, so Carter started across the grass. "Are they alright?" he asked Linda again.

It was probably some kids messing around, daring each other to do stupid shit.

"They are. But Ken has her at knifepoint."

Carter stopped walking. *"Ken has Bridgett at knifepoint?"* Carter started jogging now.

"Not Bridgett. She called it in. He's got the perp at knifepoint."

"The perp is a woman?"

He wasn't sexist. He really wasn't. But the chances of a break-in in Bad were a thousand to one, and the chance of it being a woman doing the breaking in were easily a million to one.

"She's a woman. And Ken's not letting her go. At this point, I'm more worried about her than them."

Carter slid behind the wheel of his truck. "Is the perp armed?"

"No. She has…cheesecake," Linda said.

Carter paused at that. "Cheesecake?"

"Chocolate apparently."

Damn, he loved chocolate cheesecake. "What the hell is going on?"

"I don't know. That's what Bridgett told me. She's also pissed because the woman is wearing a trench coat over lingerie and high heels. I think *Ken* might be the one in danger in between the two women."

"Ken's cheating?" Carter asked. He let up on the gas a bit. This didn't sound quite as ominous, suddenly.

Ken and Bridgett were in their late forties and had been married for probably twenty-some years by now. In Carter's experience, that meant that Ken had definitely cheated. More than once.

But Ken was thirty pounds overweight, balding, and generally a really nice guy. There was no way was he going to knife his mistress.

"If he is, his girlfriend is going to be pissed," Linda said. "Maybe she showed up when Bridgett was supposed to be gone or something, but now Ken's got her on the other end of a butcher knife and claims to have never seen her before."

Carter was glad the people at the reception hadn't heard all of *these* details. There would have been a crowd on the street in front of the house in ten minutes.

"Do you still have Bridgett on the line?" he asked, turning onto Maple Street.

"Yep."

"Tell her to have Ken stand down. I'm here."

"You got it."

Two minutes later, he pulled up in front of the house.

He approached the front door, taking in the scene around him quickly.

There was no sign of forced entry. Which, with cheesecake in hand, would have been difficult anyway, Carter thought dryly.

But that meant she had a key, or someone had let her in.

Provided she'd come through the front.

Once he had the knife out of Ken's hand and figured out who the hell this woman was, he could worry about how she'd gotten in the house.

"Ken?" Carter called as he opened the unlocked front door. "Bridgett?"

"In the dining room!" Bridgett answered.

Carter headed in that direction. As he stepped through the doorway, he found about what he'd expected. Bridgett was standing behind Ken, her arms crossed, looking pissed off. Ken had the other woman backed into the corner and was still holding the damned butcher knife, but at least it was at his side rather than at anyone's throat. All Carter could see of the other woman were her shoes—black, four-inch heels— her ankles and the hem of the trench coat Linda had mentioned.

There was also chocolate cheesecake all over the floor.

Which was, frankly, a travesty.

"Knife on the table, Ken," Carter said firmly. "Let's get this worked out."

Ken turned and tossed the knife on the dining room table. "Fine. But I want to make a statement."

"Not until I do," Bridgett said.

"Everyone gets to make a statement," Carter said, pulling out his notebook. He leaned to look around Ken at the other woman, but she scooted to the side as he did, hiding behind Ken's taller and wider frame.

Carter frowned. "*Everyone* will make a statement," he repeated. "I assume this was some kind of misunderstanding?"

"I understand perfectly," Bridgett said.

"No, you don't," Ken told her. "She isn't here for me."

"Was anything taken? Any damage done?" Carter asked, stepping to the side to try to get a look at the woman behind Ken. But she moved again. "Besides the cheesecake, of course," Carter said, trying to lighten the moment.

"Oh, I'd say there's some damage done," Bridgett said, her voice cold. "As in the ruin of a twenty-four-year marriage."

Carter winced.

"Jesus Christ!" Ken bellowed. "She isn't here for me!"

"Then why the hell is she in my house in next to nothing

with cheesecake, Ken?" Bridgett yelled back. "I was supposed to be at the wedding reception tonight and you were 'working late'." Bridgett made air quotes with her fingers. "I'm sure she just walked into the wrong house."

"I have never seen this woman before in my life!" Ken told her. "*She* told you that she got the wrong house."

Okay, that was enough.

"Ken, can you step over here please?" Carter asked.

Ken stomped to Carter's side.

"This isn't what it looks like. And I wasn't going to hurt her. I was protecting my home and family. I didn't know she wasn't armed and there was no way I was touching her to pat her down for weapons. Not dressed like that. Bridgett would have cut my balls off. And you can't arrest me for the knife," Ken told him.

But Carter barely heard him.

Because Ken might not know the woman in the trench coat.

But Carter did.

"*Lacey?*"

She sighed and met his eyes. "Hi, Carter."

How in the *hell*…

It was the wedding. Had to be. Like a spell had been cast over everything around him, making him nostalgic and soft and stupid. And fucking everything up.

Carter just stared.

But wedding spell or not, Lacey Andrews was definitely standing in front of him. In a trench coat. With his favorite dessert at her feet.

CHAPTER
TWO

"YOU KNOW HER?" Bridgett demanded.

"I *told you* I got the wrong house," Lacey said.

"You were trying to find *his* house?" Bridgett asked. She turned wide eyes to Carter.

"You were trying to find *my* house?" Carter repeated dumbly.

Of course, Lacey didn't know anyone else in Bad.

The trench coat—and the reports of lingerie underneath—were definitely throwing him off though.

"Yes. I thought this was your house. I was going to…surprise you."

Her cheeks flushed and Carter felt a stirring beneath his belt.

He'd made Lacey blush a number of times in the past.

Long in the past.

Okay, not *that* long. The last time had been twelve months ago.

To the day.

It wasn't that he hadn't realized what day it was. He'd just been staunchly ignoring it. And blaming his shitty mood on the wedding.

The wedding was part of it, no question. But today was also Lacey's birthday.

He knew because he'd helped her celebrate it last year.

Right before he'd completely ruined it.

And the things that had transpired since then were... unbelievable, actually. And painful. Very fucking painful.

"Why?" That was all he could come up with at the moment.

"I needed to see you."

"Today."

She nodded. "Especially today."

Because she was sad. And lonely. And grieving.

He ran a hand through his hair. He'd been proud of himself for only thinking about what today was every other hour. The day was almost over. Another three hours and he would have made it through. Without calling her or getting drunk or anything else self-destructive.

And now she was standing here in front of him.

In a damned trench coat with lingerie underneath and chocolate cheesecake at her feet.

Suddenly anger and frustration coursed through him. Neither were new in regards to this situation and how he felt about Lacey, but he'd only seen her in person once since he'd admitted the devastating truth—that he'd fallen in love with her.

He wasn't sure how to handle facing her now.

The only time he'd seen her in person since being knocked on his ass by that unwelcome revelation had been at Garrett's funeral ten months ago.

He crossed the space between them before he'd really thought about what he was doing. He grasped her by the upper arm and started for the door. She tripped along on her heels, trying to hold the front of the coat shut and keep up with his long strides at the same time.

The sound of someone clearing their throat, made him stop.

Belatedly, he remembered that there were two more people in the room.

He looked at Ken and Bridgett. "Do you want to press charges?"

They were both staring at Lacey and him with wide eyes.

Bridgett shook her head slowly. Ken said, "Uh, no, we're good."

Apparently they believed that Lacey was here to see Carter after all.

"Fine."

He started for the door again, not trusting himself to look at Lacey when they were this close.

It was bad enough that he could smell her.

She smelled like jasmine.

She'd always smelled like jasmine.

He marched her through the Logans' front door, down the steps, across the grass, and up the porch steps to his own front door.

He paused and dug for his keys, still holding her arm.

"Where are we—" she started.

He unlocked the door and shoved it open, nudging her through.

"Oh."

"You almost got it right." He was amazed that his voice sounded as calm as it did.

"Oops."

He hit the switch on the wall, bathing the foyer in a soft light.

And finally looked at Lacey.

She gave him a small, wobbly smile.

Fuck.

He wanted her with every fiber of his being.

"What are you doing here?"

He realized he hadn't let go of her yet, but he couldn't quite bring himself to do it now either. He was only holding her arm and it wasn't even skin to skin, but he hadn't touched her in twelve months. Not even when they'd both been grieving Garrett. The last time he'd touched her had definitely been skin to skin and it had changed his life.

Yeah, he wasn't quite up to letting her go just yet.

Then she licked her lips. And Carter realized not letting go of her was a huge error in judgement.

Everything in his body tightened and he had to consciously keep his hand from squeezing her arm too hard.

"I had to see you," she said. Her voice wavered slightly. "I'm sorry. I shouldn't have surprised you."

"Or my neighbors."

She nodded. "Right."

"So why did you? Why didn't you call?"

They were standing too close. He was touching her, smelling her, feeling the warmth of her body reaching out to him.

He hadn't been this close to her since that night. That night. The best, most horrible, most amazing, awful night of his life.

"I didn't think you would want me to come," she said softly. "I thought showing up without warning you was a better idea."

"I don't like surprises." That was an understatement.

"But you won't throw me out."

Her voice wasn't wavering now. She wasn't blushing now. She was meeting his eyes directly. Like she knew him.

And she did.

Because no, he wouldn't throw her out. Or, more accurately, he *couldn't*.

Not because he was a cop and his job was to serve and protect. Not because he was a nice guy—definitely not that. But because he was a selfish ass who wanted her more than he wanted his sanity.

Apparently.

He turned and pressed her back against the door and moved in until he could feel the length of her body against his.

"Say no if you're going to say no," he said gruffly.

Her breath caught, her pupils dilated and her lips parted.

"Lace. This is your last chance."

But she didn't say no.

She didn't say yes.

What she said was much, much worse.

"Please, Carter."

———

Lacey saw Carter's eyes darken and his jaw tighten. She felt his fingers dig into her arm. But then he breathed in through his nose and pressed closer and she knew that neither of them was leaving that door with all their clothes on.

Thank *God.*

That was exactly what she needed. Exactly why she was here.

"Why?" he asked.

Just one little word.

She frowned. What? He was asking questions? She hadn't expected him to keep talking. She squeezed her eyes shut and tipped her head back against the door.

He was hot and hard and *there.* It had been so long since she'd been held, since she'd been touched, since she'd just lost herself to *good* sensations. She'd been overcome by many, many bad ones in the past ten months. She really needed to feel something good.

Carter Shaw was the only man who could make her feel good again.

And she really, really wanted to feel good.

"Lacey?"

She felt him start to shift back and her eyes flew open and she grabbed the front of his shirt. "No!" He couldn't leave her.

His eyes were full of concern as he lifted a hand and brushed her hair back from her face. "What's going on?"

"It's my birthday," she said simply. "You're my present to myself."

Nothing about this was simple.

And yet, it really was.

She missed Garrett and Carter. So she was here to see the one she could still see.

Carter had been a big part of her relationship with Garrett, and avoiding Carter over the past ten months because he reminded her too much of Garrett had felt as if she'd lost them both at once.

It was her fault that she hadn't seen or talked to Carter. She'd kept him at a distance by not calling him after Garrett had been shot and not going to him when he'd shown up at the funeral. But one word from him and she would have been in the corner in a fetal position. She'd barely been holding it together as it was. And she'd known that if she didn't go to him, Carter wouldn't come to *her*. Demanding she see or talk to him wasn't Carter's style. She'd known that he would leave her completely alone when she'd avoided even eye contact with him at the funeral.

But it had been ten months.

And now she needed him.

She wanted the reminder of Garrett now. The three of them had always had a strange, amazing, fun, comfortable relation-ship. And she missed it. She ached with missing it. It had made her whole and she needed as much of it back as she could get.

The two men together had made a single perfect man. And they'd both been hers. Kind of. She'd only had Carter once a month or so when he came to town to hang out for the weekend. And Garrett had been the only one sharing her bed every night. But Carter really *felt* like a boyfriend when he was around. Other than the sleeping-with-other-women thing. But he held doors and bought her gifts and called her randomly from time to time and they would talk until the sun came up. It had been so...strange.

And Garrett had never minded. Nor had Carter ever seemed jealous of where she spent her nights. While she had, at times, been jealous of Carter's other women.

But none were serious—Carter didn't do serious—so it was hard to get too worked up when they were never around for more than a couple of weeks. And, of course, when she was sleeping with Garrett.

She'd met the men at the same time. Literally. They'd both

come up to her together at a wedding reception they were all attending. They'd been openly competing for her attention. She'd danced and drank and flirted with both of them. But by the end of the night, Carter had told her that Garrett was a great guy and she should give him her number. She'd taken that as a sign that Carter wasn't into her for more than a one-night flirtation.

Yet he'd been around, a part of her relationship with Garrett from then on. It had never felt odd, had never felt like one too many people at dinner or in the conversation or even on the couch when they'd watched movies. She'd put her head in Garrett's lap and her feet in Carter's and they would snuggle like an old married couple...of three.

The guys couldn't have been more different. Garrett had been the big, spontaneous, outgoing and fun guy. He'd been tall and blond and loud. Carter was the serious, intense, scary-intelligent one. He had dark hair and eyes and was about an inch shorter than Garrett's 6'3". But both men kept in excellent shape as cops. Both were wide and solid, strong, and gorgeous.

She'd always thought she had a type before she met them, but it was impossible to say which was better looking and while she loved spending time alone with Garrett, when Carter was with them things felt, somehow, complete in a way it didn't when he wasn't there.

It was as if the men were two halves of a whole.

And now Garrett was gone and she hadn't seen Carter in ten months.

That was wrong. She couldn't lose them both.

She'd had everything a woman could want with the two men. Garrett had been fun and crazy and could always make her laugh. He had been the one she needed to make her kick back and relax. Garrett had been the one she wanted to tell good news to. He'd whoop it up and celebrate and tell her she was amazing.

Carter was the one she wanted to talk to about her mom's depression and the one she could talk politics with. Carter was the one she told bad news first. Carter had never whooped in his life, but he always made her feel better when things weren't going well. He never said the words "you are amazing" but she somehow sensed that he thought so.

When Garrett forgot that she didn't like onions on her pizza, Carter would pick them off before he served her. When Carter forgot her birthday, Garrett had it covered. With a big party. Or an even bigger surprise. Like last year when Garrett had suggested something she'd stupidly—and drunkenly—confessed to wanting.

The thing that had broken up his and Carter's friendship.

And her and Carter's friendship.

Lacey pulled in a deep, shaky breath.

"Lacey, I know you're hurting." Carter's voice was tight.

"Don't you miss him?" she asked hoarsely. "Don't you have this huge gaping hole in your life with him gone?"

Carter was clearly in pain when he said, "Jesus, Lace, I miss him every fucking day."

"I need to miss him *with* you," she said, not knowing what her words were going to be for sure before she said them. "I can't do this on my own anymore. I can't miss you both. It's crazy for *us* to be apart just because he's gone, isn't it?"

Carter studied her face so intently that she had to wonder what he was looking for—or what he was seeing.

She loved him. It felt weird to say that without Garrett a part of the equation, but it was true. She felt guilty about it. She'd planned to marry Garrett. A girl couldn't just fall into the arms of the would-have-been-fiancé's best friend.

But she did love Carter. Being with him, seeing him, talking to him felt better than anything had in a long time.

"I've almost called you a million times," he finally said. "I've missed you so damned much. I've worried about you. I've wondered about you."

A huge breath left Lacey's body at that and she felt the relief pour through her. "Thank God." She leaned in and wrapped her arms around him. "Hold me."

His arms went around her immediately as well and he pulled her into his body.

For a moment they just stood like that, pressed together. Then Carter's hand started stroking up and down her back and she felt the tension in her muscles begin to melt. She buried her face against his neck and breathed in his beloved, familiar scent.

It had been so long. She and Carter had always been comfortable touching one another—hugs, foot or neck rubs, his hand at her back if they were maneuvering through a crowd—but the last time had been that night. Her birthday. The night Garrett had given her the birthday present he'd been teasing about for weeks.

He'd encouraged Carter to kiss her. *Really* kiss her. And had suggested the threesome. The thing she'd had dirty dreams about. The thing he'd gotten her to admit when they'd been sharing their deepest fantasies.

They'd all had too much too drink. They'd all been having such a good time. It was her birthday after all. So Carter had done it. He'd kissed her. Deeply. Hot and dirty. God, it had been so good.

Then he'd started touching her. He'd undressed her.

And then he'd stopped.

But she still remembered how he'd looked at her for those several long, hot, breathtaking moments. She'd seen the emotions swirling in his eyes.

And how, without a word, he'd turned, stomped out of the bedroom, down the stairs, and slammed out of the house.

That had been the last time she'd seen Carter for nearly two months.

The next had been across the room at Garrett's funeral.

Carter hadn't come to Baton Rouge again after that night. He hadn't called or texted her.

Garrett had gone after him. She'd heard their raised voices in the driveway, but she'd sat on the end of the bed and purpose-fully *not* listened to what they were saying.

After he came back inside, she and Garrett had gone to bed. Without touching. Without talking about what had happened. After that, Garrett hadn't even mentioned the fact that he hadn't seen Carter in months. She hadn't brought it up either.

She and Garrett had been okay after that. Things had been mostly normal. They'd seen each other all the time, laughed and made love.

And a week later, Garrett had gotten down on one knee and proposed.

She'd said yes.

They'd acted like a happily-in-love, newly engaged couple planning their future.

But something had been missing.

"Damn you." She pulled back swiftly from Carter's embrace to scowl at him.

He looked confused. "What?"

"I *missed* you," she said.

His expression softened. "I've missed you too. I know the funeral—"

"Not just that. I missed you long before that. You were always there, even when you weren't there you were *there*. We talked, we had…*something*. And then that night…then it was all different and…I *missed* you. I lost you that night. And then I lost him."

She didn't realize that she'd started crying until Carter lifted a hand and brushed a tear off her cheek with his thumb.

"I know," he said simply.

"And I did miss you at the funeral," she said. "I'm sorry about that."

He nodded. "I understood."

She shook her head. She wasn't sure he did. "You remind me of him. And it was so painful. But *he* reminded me of *you*. That was painful too. And I think *I* reminded him of you, and…" She trailed off.

She and Garrett had never even been back to their favorite restaurant because it was where they always went when Carter was in town. But neither of them had ever suggested it. It was as if neither of them even wanted to bring it up. "It was like *you* had died after…that night."

She said the last two words on a whisper as her entire body flushed. Looking into his eyes, with one of his hands on her face and one on her hip, thinking back to her birthday night made feelings and memories wash over with a speed that made her head spin. Lust and embarrassment and regret and hurt.

She pulled back, overwhelmed with emotions.

Carter dropped his hand, as if reading what was going through her mind. As if it was really her mind at play here.

It felt a lot more like her body. And her heart.

He tucked his hands into his pockets and just looked at her.

Lacey put her palms against her hot cheeks. "God, I'm sorry. I don't know what's wrong with me."

"You're remembering that night," he said.

Even those few words made hot sparks of desire shoot to her core. *She* had said "that night" but hearing him refer to it, in that deep voice that seemed to rumble through her more as a physical feeling than an auditory sensation, made her go weak and hot.

"I think about it all the time," she heard herself admit.

His gaze burned into hers. "So do I."

She'd thought so. Hoped so. But hadn't been sure. Carter had been with a lot of women, in a lot of ways.

"That night never should have happened," Carter said hoarsely. "I should have said no."

She sucked in a breath. "You *did* say no."

They hadn't had sex. He'd stopped before that. Even though Garrett was okay with it. Even though *she* was okay with it. Her cheeks burned even now thinking about *how* okay she'd been. She'd been absolutely wanton. Two years ago, before meeting Garrett and Carter, if someone had told her she'd be wanting to, *intending to*, have sex with two men at once, she would have adamantly denied it. That was so not her. But with those two—yeah, she'd been all in.

But Carter had stopped it. He'd kissed her and touched her through her clothes and undressed her…and then stopped.

"I should have said no to all of it. I shouldn't have even kissed you."

Her cheeks burned even hotter now. Lacey felt her eyes widen and her heart pounded. She started shaking her head and stepped forward. "Don't say that. God, please don't say that."

Carter's expression was tight as he took a deep breath. "If that night hadn't happened, things would have stayed the same. I wouldn't have stopped talking to my best friend two months before he died."

Lacey frowned slightly. "*You're* the one who changed it. You're the one who left."

"I couldn't share you, Lace."

The air sucked out of her lungs.

He pinned her with an intense stare. "I knew it before that night, but that was the night when I *knew* that I couldn't keep going while he was with you. I couldn't share you and I couldn't watch him have you. He was my best friend, but I couldn't watch him have what I wanted so fucking much. Not like *that* certainly, but in any way. I know it made me the ultimate asshole, but I had to leave."

Tears burned her eyes.

Garrett was gone now. He didn't have her now.

She knew there were all kinds of complicated emotions around that, but it was their reality. And she was so fucking tired of being sad and alone and without Carter.

"I'm here now," she said, spreading her arms wide. The coat was buttoned up so only the top gaped. But it was enough to show the edge of the electric-blue bustier. "I need you, Carter.

No one else can help me feel what I need to. I want to feel the way I always did when I was with you."

His gaze took her in from the top of her head to the tips of her shoes. But he didn't move. Didn't make a sound.

God, she wanted him. And not just the sex, though forgetting every other emotion for a while and just letting herself get wrapped up and washed away in pleasure sounded damn good. But she needed the connection that only Carter could give her. The *connection* that had been there even before Garrett had decided to surprise her for her twenty-seventh birthday with the fulfillment of her ultimate fantasy—confessed to him when she'd been drunk on Bacardi and playing Truth or Dare with him and Carter.

She remembered sitting on the floor around their square coffee table one night when Carter had come to town, drinking shots that included rum, coconut liqueur and chocolate syrup, and talking. The shots had eventually morphed into taking shots of the rum straight out of the bottle, and the conversation had morphed into a dangerous game.

Garrett had asked her if she'd ever consider a threesome. She'd said yes. And then he'd asked her who the third would be.

She remembered, in spite of her fuzzy-headed state, looking straight at Carter and saying, "Only Carter".

She also remembered the look on Carter's face—a mix of heat, need, and dread.

Her birthday hadn't been for three more months and she'd almost forgotten about the conversation. Almost. Except for every time Carter was in town after that.

But Garrett hadn't forgotten. And the night of her birthday they'd taken her out for dinner and then they'd gone dancing at a club. And Carter had danced with her. Typically, he danced, but not with her. Garrett was her only partner on the dance floor. Until that night.

That's when she'd wondered.

And when they'd walked to the car with her in between

them, it felt more intimate than usual. They were both always protective of her and she was always put in the middle, but they both had their hands on her that night. Garrett had been holding her hand and Carter's hand had been on her lower back all the way to the car.

So she hadn't been shocked that Carter had been standing in the doorway when Garrett led her straight to the bedroom and kissed her deeply and told her that he always wanted to make all of her dreams come true.

"I'd planned to seduce you tonight," she said.

"I see."

"You're not looking seduced, suddenly."

He sighed. "I wish it was that easy."

"It is. It can be." Lacey stepped forward and grabbed the front of his shirt again. "I need you, Carter. I need to be with you."

His gaze went from her eyes to her mouth, then back up.

He didn't touch her. He didn't have to. She felt the heat.

"Do you know why I told you to give Garrett your phone number that first night?" he asked, instead of grabbing her and kissing her senseless as she'd been hoping.

"Because he was one of your best friends and you cared about him and…" She hesitated. She didn't want to sound like a child. She knew that Carter had liked that she wasn't clingy and needy and whiny like so many of the women he dated. Or so he told her and Garrett. It seemed like whenever they all talked about Carter's girlfriends, he started off with something like "not all women are like you, Lacey" or "I wish there were more women like you". Yet, he'd told her to go for his best friend.

"And?" he prompted, one eyebrow up.

"He liked me more than you did."

Something flared in Carter's eyes and his brows slammed together. "No," he said firmly. "That was not it."

She tugged him closer and he took a step forward. "Then why?"

She'd always wondered. It was actually kind of amazing that, in all of the times the three of them had shared their secrets and dreams, in all of the times they'd gotten tipsy and their tongues had gotten loose sitting around Garrett's fireplace or out on the deck looking at the stars, she hadn't asked this question.

But she hadn't really wanted to hear him say that he hadn't felt about her the way Garrett did.

It shouldn't matter. She'd had Garrett. She'd been happy with him and it was wonderful that he was the one she'd given her number to. Garrett had been fun and had made her feel like a princess. He'd spoiled her and showed her he loved her in big ways.

Carter was more serious. He was the quieter one, for sure, but he also seemed to just always be observing, taking everything in. He made her feel special in different ways. Where Garrett was openly demonstrative and said how he felt easily and often, Carter seemed…harder. As if getting close to him would be difficult. So knowing that he let her close was something she cherished.

"Because he could give you what you needed," Carter said.

"What does that mean?" But she knew.

"You're a romantic, Lacey. You want the big gestures and the pretty words and the sweet, fun stuff. Garrett is—was—that guy."

Maybe if he hadn't stumbled over the is/was thing. Maybe if his voice hadn't gotten gruff there. Maybe if she hadn't seen the pain in his eyes, she would have let it go. Because she knew that was true. With Garrett there had been a future. Not so with Carter.

But he did stumble and his hurt over losing Garrett was obvious, so all she could do was press against him, wrap her arms around his neck, and whisper against his lips, "All I need is *you* tonight."

LACEY WANTED him because she was sad and lonely. Lacey was the girlfriend-type, not the hot-weekend-fling type. Lacey had been the love of his best friend's life.

Another man might have thought of all those things and resisted sliding one hand to the back of her neck, his other hand to her ass, and sealing his mouth over hers.

Carter was not that man.

Carter kissed her deeply, drinking in the feel of her lips, the scent of her skin, the way she arched closer and gripped his shoulders and moaned. He urged her mouth open and stroked her bottom lip, then her tongue with his. He pressed her against his cock and ground into her sweet softness.

Lacey Andrews was everything he'd always wanted if he'd let himself want things like forever. And right now she was in his arms asking him for something he absolutely could give her.

She needed sex? She needed to *feel* again? She needed to remember what it was like to have a man want her and take care of her and make her cry with pleasure instead of grief?

He was *that* man.

He kissed her with every bit of need and loss he'd felt over the past twelve months. He kissed her as if he was never going to have another chance in his life.

Carter felt her hands at the front of his shirt, working on the buttons, and shuddered. He needed her hands on him. He needed to be against every inch of her. She might be here because she was sad and lonely, but he'd wanted to soothe those things for her ten months ago and because he hadn't been able to do it, there had been a hard knot of regret in his gut since. Now she was here, and making her feel good, making her forget for a little while, was as healing for him as it would be for her.

He let her lips go, trailing his mouth over her cheek to her ear. "I need to see under this coat, Lace."

She was still working on his buttons when she said, "I know you like blue."

He pulled back to see her face. "Did you buy this for me?"

She bit her bottom lip and nodded.

Fuck yeah you did.

He was going to have all kinds of mixed emotions later, he knew, but he didn't give a shit at the moment. Lacey was here in sexy *blue* underwear. For him.

All for him.

He wasn't sending her to bed with another man after an evening of laughing and talking. He wasn't going upstairs to his bed alone. Or with a woman who was supposed to fill the void in his life that came from having everything with Lacey but her body.

She was *his* tonight.

Yeah, a better man might have sent her to bed alone—at the bed-and-breakfast in town.

But Carter wasn't that man either.

He stepped back. His shirt was completely open and he loved the way her gaze roamed over his chest and down his abs hungrily. He wasn't too proud to soak all of that in.

Carter shrugged out of his shirt and tossed it toward the

living room. Then he reached out and grabbed the end of the belt that wrapped around her coat. He tugged it loose.

"Unbutton for me," he told her.

He could see that she was breathing raggedly but she went right for the buttons without hesitation. He knew she was thinking of nothing but the two of them and what was about to happen, and he was going to make damned sure that she didn't think of anything else until the sun came up.

The V neck had already given him a hint of the blue satin underneath but as the buttons gave and the coat parted, Carter found it impossible to swallow. Or even breathe deep.

It wasn't a teddy. It was a bustier and tiny silk panties. *Only* a bustier and tiny silk panties.

The coat opened and Lacey shrugged it off, letting it pool at her feet.

Her feet looked amazing in the high black heels, but he couldn't make himself move his gaze past about mid-thigh. There was just so much to look at.

The bustier pushed her breasts higher, the tops of the gorgeous curves peeking out from the top of the bright blue satin. Black laces crisscrossed over her rib cage and hugged her waist. There was a strip of smooth, bare skin between the bottom of the bustier and the top of her panties that Carter intended to drag his tongue over thoroughly.

But the most breathtaking sight was when he again focused on her face and saw the raw desire in her eyes. She stood and let him look and his eyes on her fired her blood. He fucking loved that.

He needed to feel how hot and wet she was for him. He needed to hear her begging him for release. He needed to feel her come around him, *for* him.

It was all for him.

"I do love blue," he said.

She gave him a small smile. "I saw it and knew—"

The rest of what she'd been about to say was lost when Carter stooped to sweep her up into his arms.

Her arms went around his neck. "Not up against the door?"

She almost sounded disappointed and Carter looked down at her. "You want me to fuck you up against the door, Lace?"

He was already throbbing and hard, but that image—and the idea that was what *she* wanted—made his cock press against his zipper painfully.

"I just didn't think you'd be able to help it," she said, her cheeks getting a little pink.

He loved making Lacey blush.

"I want you spread out on my bed," he told her honestly. "Just like I've imagined so damned many times. I want to watch you squirming against my sheets and see you grab onto my headboard as I thrust into you and I want to smell your shampoo on my pillow in the morning. But if you want the door—"

"No, bed. Now." Her eyes were wide and the pink in her cheeks was now obviously from arousal.

Carter felt a surge of satisfaction. Everything he'd said was true. He'd imagined all of those things with her, many painful times. But he also couldn't forget that Lacey was a romantic. Those weren't the most poetic words ever uttered by a man to a woman, but that was as close as he was likely to get and Lacey probably knew that.

No, she *did* know that. She knew him. And she was here in his house in underwear she'd bought for him anyway.

Carter started for the stairs.

"And the door another time," she said.

He almost stumbled on the step. He looked down at her. She was giving him a mischievous, sexy smile that almost stopped his heart.

He had no idea what kind of lover Lacey was, he realized. He'd kissed her *once*, on a night orchestrated by her boyfriend, who had been there the whole time, and Carter hadn't even undressed before he'd had to escape. Still, it had been the hottest and sweetest night of his life.

But that had been Lacey's first even sort-of-almost-a-three-some so had been unusual for her, obviously. Carter didn't know if she was typically a vixen or submissive or adventurous. Maybe it seemed that the threesome made her adventurous, but he knew the night the three of them had shared had nothing to do with being wild or daring. A threesome with anyone else, yes. But the three of *them* was different. In so many ways, it had felt like he and Garrett had both been dating her all along.

No, being with him and Garrett together hadn't been daring for Lacey. It had seemed inevitable.

For Carter it had been…life-changing.

Just kissing this woman and seeing her naked had ruined him.

He'd had other women since then but none had truly satis-fied him. His short-term relationships had become even shorter and less meaningful. He'd been restless and unhappy.

And Carter had changed things between the three of them when he'd walked out. Because Garrett had finally realized that his best friend was truly *in love* with his girlfriend.

Then Garrett had proposed to her. And taken her away from Carter forever.

Then Garrett had gotten shot.

And forever had taken on a new, horrible meaning.

Until now. Lacey was here, in his arms, about to be in his bed, and no matter what that said about Carter and his character or whatever, he was taking this night.

He'd deal with the guilt and consequences tomorrow.

He strode to his bedroom, hit the light and crossed to the bed, where he dropped her onto the mattress. Her hair spread out over his white sheets, the blue of her underwear bright against the plain linens.

"Fuck, you're gorgeous," he told her, unbuckling his belt and throwing it toward the dresser.

She propped up on her elbows, her eyes on his face rather than on his fly as he unbuttoned and unzipped. But he didn't push his pants off just yet. He had a lot to do, a lot of time to make up for, and he couldn't be naked and maintain any control.

He put a knee on the mattress next to her and ran a hand up one silky thigh. "I know we shouldn't rush into this but I can't *not* touch you, Lacey."

"Rush?" She gave a little laugh. "I've known you for almost two years, Carter. I know you better than I know anyone. And it's been twelve long, horrible months without you. We're not rushing anything." She put her hand against his stomach. His muscles tensed under her touch and he leaned into the contact.

"Your hand feels so good on me," he told her.

"I agree." She ran her hand across his abs, along the top of his waistband. "God, I need this, Carter."

"Sex I can do. As much as you want, for as long as you need it," he said honestly. Maybe he was trying to remind her that it couldn't be more. Or maybe he was trying to remind himself.

Garrett had been the one to fulfill all of Lacey's romantic needs. Carter had been...the one to make her feel better after a shitty day at work or to talk to about the latest James Patterson novel. The third in their friendship. Yet, he'd never felt like a third wheel.

"Please make me feel good," she said. "That's what I need. To remember how to feel good."

That he could do.

He leaned in and kissed her as he drew his hand up her thigh and over the blue silk between her legs, to the smooth strip of skin above her panties. He trailed his lips down her throat, over the top of her right breast, down to the same strip of skin. He kissed her there and then licked.

She arched closer to his mouth, her hand going to his head.

"Carter," she whispered.

His name on her lips was one of the best things in his life.

He licked again, slipping a finger under the edge of her

panties and running it along the elastic from hip to the crease where her thigh and outer pussy lips met. "So hot," he breathed against her.

Lacey parted her thighs, a blatant invitation. But he wasn't done just touching and tasting yet. He lifted his head. "Fasteners in back or front?" he asked, studying the bustier.

"Back," she told him breathlessly.

He moved his hands to reach under her and loved the little whimper of protest from her. He found the tiny hooks and quickly opened them.

The bustier loosened and gaped and Carter paused for a heartbeat, relishing the moment before he saw her bare.

He apparently paused too long because Lacey pushed the corset off, letting it fall to the floor.

Carter drank in the sight.

She had smallish breasts with tight pink centers. Her skin was smooth, a gorgeous golden color with the exception of the tiny pale heart on the upper curve of her left breast. Clearly she'd been lying in the sun in nothing but a little heart sticker.

He ran a finger over the heart.

"Nude sunbathing?"

She smiled up at him. "My new loft has a private balcony."

"I promise you there are guys with binoculars trained on that private balcony."

She was so beautiful. And none of her body made him harder than the smile she gave him.

She shrugged. "I love the feeling of the hot sun touching every inch of me," she said. "I don't care if someone's looking."

He did.

The thought snuck up on him. But the idea of another man looking at this body, fantasizing about her, made a primitive streak of possessiveness go through him.

"You don't care?" he asked, leaning in to kiss the heart.

"I actually kind of like it," she admitted.

"You like the idea of some stranger seeing you naked,

watching you while he jerks off?" He moved his mouth closer to her nipple and kissed again.

She squirmed. "Maybe a little."

She had a dirty streak. Discovering that had been a slow process. When they'd first met and had been getting to know each other, all he'd seen was the sweet girl who was focused on making the world a better place. But slowly as they'd hung out, and drank together, and she and Garrett had gotten closer and more intimate, little things had started slipping out. She'd started swearing more—she tried very hard to not let the dirty words out. She'd started making innuendos, which had graduated to outright flirting that had gotten naughtier and naughtier as they'd gotten more comfortable with each other. It was always teasing, of course, but it had affected him every time.

Then Garrett had started talking.

He told Carter way more than Carter wanted to know about what Lacey was like in the bedroom. But Carter had never told him to stop. He'd felt like a total pervert but he'd been equally tortured and turned on by Garrett's stories.

He and Garrett had shared women twice before. Both times it had been hot and fun. And one night. Nothing serious. It had never occurred to Carter that Garrett would even consider sharing the woman he was in love with.

Carter hesitated. Was Garrett always going to be in his head when he was with Lacey? And did it make him a complete asshole to *not* want that? Garrett had always been a part of them before. He was the reason Carter and Lacey knew one another so well. If Garrett hadn't shared her—the dinners and laughter and weekend getaways and friendship—Carter never would have fallen in love with her.

And Garrett was the reason Lacey was here now.

Carter didn't know how to fucking feel. Should he feel grateful? Guilty?

"Carter."

Lacey's soft voice pulled his attention back to her.

Her hair, a light brown with streaks of gold from the same sun that had kissed her skin, lay around her in a wild array on his pillow. *His* pillow. Not Garrett's pillow.

She was here with him. Her choice.

Because Garrett was gone.

Carter pushed back, locking his elbows and sucking in a hard breath.

Fuck. He couldn't do this.

He stared at her for a moment, calling himself all kinds of fool, but finally he pushed up off of her and sat next to her, facing the bottom of the bed.

She didn't move for a moment, as if stunned. Finally, he felt her shift and the sheet tug as she pulled it up over herself.

"What's going on?"

There was a long moment of silence and with his eyes shut, he was all the more aware of the heat coming from her body, only inches away, and the scent of her. He should roll her all over the bed once, just to get that scent soaked deep into his sheets.

Of course, he might never leave his bed then.

Carter felt his chest and throat get tight. Son of a bitch. He'd never cried in bed. For fuck's sake. Lacey was the last person he wanted to break down in front of. And yet, she was the only person who he could imagine doing it with.

"I was *really* pissed at him, Lace," Carter finally managed.

He felt her hand on his back and he shuddered. Her touch made him hard and hot and full of want, but it was different this time. He wanted to get closer but not because of the physical release he needed.

"Pissed? Why?"

Fuck. He did *not* want to talk about this. He'd thought about it every day for the past year. But she deserved to know.

He took a deep breath. "Did he tell you what we talked about after I left?"

"No." Her voice was quiet. "I assumed he'd tell me if it was good. Or something I should know."

Carter nodded. "Okay. Well, you should know."

He felt the tension in her body. "Okay."

"He came after me asking what happened. Because before the bedroom, before that moment, I was *in*." Carter looked over at her. "I mean it, Lace. I wanted you so damned bad and I figured if that was the only way I could have you, then yeah…I was in."

She swallowed. "So what happened?"

He lifted a shoulder. "Just like a switch flipped, I was looking at you, looking so fucking gorgeous it hurt, standing next to the bed you shared with him, knowing he was right there too and…I couldn't do it. I couldn't share you. And I couldn't believe that *he* could either."

She pressed her lips together, studying his eyes. "I *wanted* it," she said softly.

"I know. We all did. On one level." He looked back at the carpet and took a shaky breath. "We'd done that before. Him and me."

"I know."

"And that was why it felt wrong, I guess. *You* were—are— different. You're not just a hot night. A fling. Even just a girlfriend."

"Is that what you talked about outside?" she asked.

"Yeah. I told him he needed to stop screwing around and take things seriously with you and that he needed to stop treating you like all the other girls." He looked over at her. "I told him I thought it was time for him to break it off."

He heard her little intake of air and her eyes widened, but he had to tell her the rest. "I told him that I didn't think he was taking your relationship seriously enough. I thought he was leaning on me to be a part of making you happy. We'd been a threesome ever since we met. And I thought it was keeping him from getting completely serious with you. I said that you deserved better than having only part of him."

She frowned, but she looked more worried than angry or hurt. "I *liked* having you as a part of us."

Carter nodded. "I know. But I was…helping him date you." He gave a short laugh. "That sounds so stupid."

Her hand ran up his back and into his hair. Her fingers slid through the short length, rubbing over his scalp. Carter sighed under the calming strokes and felt a little of the tension leave his shoulders.

"I know what you mean," she said after a moment.

Carter turned his head to look at her. "You do?"

"You guys were like two halves of a whole perfect man."

He slowly nodded. "I told him he needed to step up and do it all in every way, and stop sharing you, even with me. Or let you go."

She just held his gaze and waited.

"I expected him to let you go."

She swallowed hard. "But he proposed instead."

Carter nodded. "And I was pissed."

"Pissed?"

"Yeah. It was a jab at me. A power move."

"How so?"

"He'd realized something that night that he'd either been ignoring or I'd been better at hiding than I thought."

"What?" she asked, her voice almost a whisper.

"That I was in love with you."

She didn't look shocked, but her lips parted as she took in a quick breath.

They just sat staring at one another for several ticks.

Then she asked, softly, "Did *you* intend to propose?"

He wanted to, but he would never do that to her. He wasn't marriage material. "No."

She flinched just slightly. "Then why did you care if he did?"

"Because that would have made you off limits to me completely, in every way. And he knew that. Being in love with you myself meant that I wasn't going to be able to continue being that third wheel, watching you two live the happily ever after, wanting you but not having you. Watching him be not enough for you. So, I was going to have to walk away completely and give up what we did have."

She pressed her lips together. "You really thought he wasn't going to be good enough for me?"

"In those few weeks right after he proposed? Yeah. I was angry and jealous."

"And then he died before you could work through all of it."

She understood him. He nodded, feeling his throat tighten. "Yeah."

"You probably would have worked through it though."

"I don't know that. I'm kind of an asshole."

"I don't think so."

"I should want you to be happy. Even if I'm not involved in it at all."

She lifted a shoulder and the sheet dipped lower, exposing the upper curves of her breasts. "You're human, Carter. It's okay to have complicated feelings about things."

He lifted his hand, cupping her face. "I missed you both so fucking much, I wanted things back to how they'd been by the next weekend."

He saw the tears that welled in her eyes.

"I finally got really drunk one night and called and left a message on his phone asking him not to marry you. To call it off. To go back to how things had been with all three of us," he confessed hoarsely.

"When?" Her voice was almost a whisper.

He swallowed, emotions nearly choking him. "The night he was shot. He was probably in the ER when I called."

She gave a choked sob and his heart twisted. He wiped the tears away with his thumbs. "We missed so much because I was a jealous, possessive, stubborn ass. And then I was a selfish dick and wanted him to change everything again for me."

She shook her head. "You have to stop. Your feelings matter...mattered... too."

"I cheated all three of us out of two months of...fun, laughter…love. I should have stayed that night. Had the hottest night of any of our lives. Just left it all alone." God, his feelings for her had just overwhelmed him that night when he'd finally *had* her.

Lacey took his face between her hands. "We have *now*. That's what we need to focus on. Garrett would want us together, Carter," she said. "He would want us to both laugh and love again, live our lives, find happiness—and he would have loved it to be with each other."

She was absolutely right. Garrett would have chosen this if he'd known he'd be gone. If he'd had cancer or some other damned thing where he'd known he didn't have all the time in the world, he would have been on the phone nagging and begging Carter to take care of Lacey.

But that was the problem. The only way for Carter to really take care of Lacey was *with* Garrett. Garrett been the romantic, fun-loving, pamper-her-and-whisk-her-off-her-feet guy. He'd been the things Carter wasn't.

Carter could love her.

He just wasn't sure he could—or should even try to— give her everything she needed and wanted.

What the fuck did he know about strong, positive relation-ships? He didn't even bother getting close to his father's wives anymore because they were gone so quickly and when they were gone, they were *gone,* completely out of their lives. Carter himself had fucked up the most positive relationship he'd ever been in—the one he'd had with Garrett.

So, he couldn't make Lacey any promises. He couldn't commit to anything. But he also wasn't strong enough to send her away. When she left, he'd let her. He'd remind himself it was a good thing. And until then he just had to be honest with her.

"You don't know how much I want to be what you need," he finally said.

There was a long pause and Carter knew that wasn't exactly what she wanted to hear. But Lacey was the most forgiving, loving person he'd ever met. Thank God she extended that to him.

"Well, how about we take one thing at a time?" she asked, running her hand up his arm to his shoulder. She pulled herself forward, sliding into his lap, letting the sheet fall away from her as she moved. "And right now I would really love a good, hard orgasm. If you don't mind."

Carter's body hadn't fully cooled, even with the talk about his dead best friend—something he'd maybe feel guilty about later. He was immediately ready to go.

"Orgasms I can do." He put his lips against hers. "Multiple."

He felt the little shiver of pleasure go through her and couldn't keep from kissing her. He put his hands flat on her back, pressing her close, letting her feel how hard he was for her. He opened his mouth on hers and felt her sigh. Their tongues stroked as he ran his hands up and down her back. Her hands cupped the back of his head, her fingers in his hair again. She was holding him tight and *that* was what sent the shiver of desire through him.

Well, that and her hot pussy against his cock.

For better or worse, he couldn't *not* possess her in every way he knew how.

"I want to taste you," he said against her mouth.

"Yes, God, Carter," she gasped.

She started to slide out of his lap, but he gripped her hips. "Like this, Lace." He lay back, urging her up his body.

"Holy crap," she said on a breath he almost couldn't hear.

"Knees by my ears, babe."

CHAPTER
FOUR

LACEY THOUGHT she was going to burn up.

There had always been something about Carter that instantly made her panties wet. When she'd met him and Garrett, she remembered looking up at Garrett and smiling and then looking at Carter and catching her breath. That was the perfect way to describe the difference between the two men. Garrett had given off a life-of-the-party vibe. Carter had given off a get-naked-right-now vibe. When she thought of Carter, she'd feel her body clench and she'd have to stifle a moan. Both feelings were strong. The memory of both men would stay with her. But the difference in how they made her feel was distinct.

She'd known plenty of good-looking, flirty guys, but good-looking and sexy were not the same thing. And she'd never describe Carter with a fun word like flirty. He was…sexy. That was all there was to it. She supposed she could have described some of their interactions as flirting. Technically. They'd teased, they'd laughed, they'd said inappropriately naughty things to each other that they'd only kind of meant. Or that they'd completely meant but hadn't expected to act on. But with Carter it didn't feel light and silly. It always felt as if there was a serious, underlying…threat.

It was liking poking a bear.

A patient bear who was a good friend and had a long fuse maybe. But she'd always wondered what it would be like when she got to the end of that fuse. And she'd kept poking.

Now they were there.

His fingers dug into her hips as he moved her over his mouth. Thankfully. She wasn't sure she could have moved on her own. Her bones felt like they were made of molten lava.

Her panties were still on, but that didn't stop Carter from pressing her against his mouth. Even that much pressure against her needy clit was enough to rip a moan from her throat. She let her head fall back and put her hands on his, seeking a way of anchoring herself to him.

Not that he gave any indication he was moving away anytime soon.

He took a long, deep breath and even as her cheeks burned, she felt herself grow wetter with the intimacy of it.

"Goddamn, you smell so fucking good," he muttered. "I could stay here for a week."

She pressed her fingers into his hands. "Need your tongue, Carter."

He groaned against her, vibrating her clit and making her grip his hands even harder.

Wow, she hadn't meant to say that. Or she had, but not out loud.

She loved sex. She was fine with asking for what she wanted.

But she sensed with Carter it was going to push beyond what she was used to. She had a feeling she was going to—and totally could—say things to Carter she hadn't to Garrett. Not because she would have shocked the other man, but because there were things she wanted from Carter that hadn't occurred to her before.

"I love these panties," he said. "But they're in my way right now. If you want them in one piece, you better move 'em over."

Lacey moved her hand right away.

She didn't really care if they stayed in one piece. She'd bought them for this night and they were getting exactly the reaction she'd hoped for, but it was hot to think about moving them out of the way for his mouth. Like she would be fully participating in the dirty act of him tonguing her to orgasm.

She pulled the panties to the side, exposing herself to him.

He groaned again and his grip didn't just tighten on her, he pulled her down against his face firmly.

His tongue met her clit in a long, hard lick that sent sparks of heat and want shooting through her body. Her nipples tightened almost painfully and she throbbed deep in her pelvis.

He licked several times, his tongue rough against her, winding her tighter and tighter, the cluster of nerve endings growing more and more sensitive. But as she was approaching the summit, he moved her, dragging his tongue lower. He licked at her opening and she couldn't gather one ounce of embarrassment over how wet she was.

"Yes, God, Lace, I love how you want this," he said gruffly against her.

"Yes. More." She simply couldn't come up with any words beyond those.

"Grind against me," he commanded huskily.

It was like her body was programmed to obey him and she immediately rocked against his mouth.

His tongue dove inside her and she cried out.

He kept at her like that for several strokes, then moved her again before she could get too close to the edge.

He shifted to get a hand between them, sliding two fingers into her as he returned to her clit.

She whimpered as need coursed through her. Falling forward slightly, she grasped his headboard, putting more pressure against her clit.

"Suck on me," she begged him. "Please."

"Fuck yes. Open up for me."

She started to react, but realized that her hand on the headboard was holding her in the *perfect* position and her other hand was still holding her panties out of the way. "I can't. I—"

With a low growl, his hands went to the seam along the side of the panties, yanking hard and ripping them off. His fingers pressed back inside her immediately and she cried out with how good the rough thrust felt against her sensitive, swollen tissues. Reacting without true thought, she reached between her legs and with two fingers, spread herself open for him.

"So good," was all she heard as he brought her down against his mouth again. He licked once, long and firm, then fastened his lips on her clit. He gave her one quick second to take a breath, and then sucked.

Her hips ground into him of their own accord and Lacey cried out his name as an orgasm slammed into her.

She was just pulling in a huge lungful of needed oxygen when Carter flipped her to her back.

"Condom?"

Lacey knew he wasn't asking if she had one, he was asking if he needed to use one. She'd been with only Garrett for almost two years, and she was on the pill for pregnancy.

"Not for me," she said. "You?"

"Clean."

"Good."

He gave her a funny look that flipped her heart for a reason she didn't understand. "I always use a condom, Lace."

"Oh, well, then—"

"But I don't want anything between us."

God, she didn't either, and she wasn't talking about a piece of latex. She didn't want the past, the regrets, even Garrett's ghost between them. Right now all she wanted was Carter. All of him. Just him.

She didn't know what all was going through Carter's mind and heart. She'd never met a man better at hiding his thoughts and feelings, and that was saying something—she'd grown up with a grandfather with clinical depression and now worked for a nonprofit mental health facility. Not that Carter had a mental illness. In fact, he had such a tight hold on his emotions that she imagined his heart had white knuckles.

But she knew there was something about her being here for him, with him, with *just* him.

She was here to fight for the love that she needed…and deserved.

She'd always been the good girl, the giver, the one to think of and do for others. She'd let Garrett and Carter decide how things would go when they'd both met her at the same time. She'd let Carter keep his distance. She'd let him pull away.

But no more.

Life was short and she did not want to leave this earth with any further regrets.

"I'm yours, Carter, however you want me," she said, choosing the words carefully. "I'll do anything for you." She meant it. There was nothing he could ask her for or demand from her that she wouldn't gladly give. She wrapped her arms around his neck and put her lips against his neck. "It's just you and me."

The groan he gave seemed to come from deep in his gut and he covered her mouth with his. The kiss was hungry and all consuming. Lacey was quickly squirming under him, seeking more. She needed him to fill her up and ease the ache—in her body and her heart.

"Take me," she whispered, using words she knew would get through any guilt or hesitation, any sense he had of protecting her. "Make me yours."

Those seemed to do the trick. He ripped his mouth from hers and pushed back onto his knees. He yanked his fly open, shoving his pants down only as far as necessary to free his cock.

"I don't want to hurt you, Lace," he said gruffly, reaching and turning her to her side.

"You won't. You can't. I want you so much, Carter." She tried to roll back, but he pinned her in position, spooning her with his big body and a strong arm around her waist.

"Take me like this the first time." He lifted her top leg and surged into her from behind.

"Oh God," she gasped. Even if it wasn't as deep and hard as it would be in another position, she felt stretched and full. So full. This was exactly what she wanted and needed. To be filled. To no longer be empty—not her time, not her home, not her bed. Not her body and not her heart.

There had been a huge missing piece in all of the above and now she was here, complete again, connected to the hard, hot body behind her.

The body that wasn't moving. Carter was holding her tightly to him, his arm like a steel band around her. He had his face buried in her hair and she felt his hot breath against the back of her neck. But he didn't move so much as his pinky finger.

She put her hand over his on her stomach. "Carter?"

"Just..." She heard him swallow hard. "Give me a second."

His voice was tight, like the words were difficult.

"Are you okay?" She wanted to turn. She wanted to see his face.

But then she felt the soft puff of air and heard his quiet laugh. "Jesus, no I'm not okay. I'm afraid if I so much as blink, I'm going to come."

She relaxed into him. Then she flexed her inner muscles around him.

He tensed—which she would have thought was impossible with how tightly he'd been holding himself.

"So you *don't* want another orgasm?" he asked, his hand twitching under hers. "Because do that again and I'm just gonna pound through my own and not worry about you, brat."

She couldn't help the little giggle that escaped. "You don't think you can get me there too? And I thought you were supposed to be this big stud in the bedroom."

Lacey barely got the words out before his hand slid down

and he pressed his middle finger against her clit. "You're playing with fire, girl," he said in a low warning voice that made her wet.

Feeling naughty and happy, and so damned grateful for feeling happy again, she squeezed him with her inner muscles. "Prove it," she taunted.

His finger started circling and she had to bite her lip to keep from moaning. He couldn't see her face either so he wouldn't know how she was reacting. She decided that this was a game she was going to have fun with. And fun was something else that had been sorely absent from her life. For just a second she was torn between crying, laughing and moaning.

But she didn't care. All of those feelings meant something she hadn't felt in far too long… she was *alive*.

"Well, that's nice, but…"

She knew the breathlessness in her voice gave her away, but Carter seemed very willing to go along with it.

"You think I don't know how to play you, Lace?" he asked huskily. "You really think that I don't know exactly how to make you go off? And you honestly think I won't do everything to make that happen before I take you hard and fast?"

Every one of the words worked for her. She loved dirty talk. More, she loved the possessiveness and barely held restraint she heard in his voice.

"Show me," she said, wiggling her ass against him, relishing the quick hiss from him.

His finger picked up the pace and his other hand, underneath her against the bed, cupped her breast. At first he just brushed over it with his thumb, but when he put his mouth against her ear and said, "You said you're all mine," he also tugged on her nipple.

She gasped, not sure if she should push forward toward his finger on her clit, or backward, against his cock.

"Say it is, Lacey. Tell me all of this is mine."

"It's all yours," she managed, feeling the orgasm winding tight.

"Which means that I can put my mouth, tongue, hands, fingers and cock anywhere I want, right?"

It was the talking. Thank God he knew that. The exact words didn't matter—all of the ones he'd just used worked great—but it was that low, gravely quality that snuck into his voice when he said them that pushed her closer and closer to the edge of bliss.

"Yes. Anywhere. Everywhere," she panted.

"Any *time* I want, right? Because it's all mine."

Mine. That one word. That was even better than fuck or cock or pussy.

"*Yes.*"

"And I can do it anywhere—here, the kitchen, the shower, the river, the hood of my car, my bike."

The reminder of his motorcycle took her *two* notches closer to her climax. She loved that thing. She'd never ridden on one until Carter, and she'd almost orgasmed right there on the seat, riding with her arms and legs around him, the wind flying past her face.

"Yes, oh please do it on your bike."

He chuckled, and the sound of it also pushed her two notches closer.

"Oh, honey, I'm going to do it in all of those places. Over and over. This sweet pussy needs lots of love."

It was such a crazy combination of dirty and sweet that she almost laughed, but then her orgasm was right there, hitting and washing over her, making her cry out and tremble in his arms.

"Fuck yes," he muttered as he began thrusting.

His deep strokes kept the ripples going and all Lacey could do was grip his arm and hang on. As promised, he didn't last long and soon he was filling her, his body shaking against hers, his breath hot against her ear.

They lay pressed tightly together, limbs entwined, for several long minutes.

Lacey had known coming to Bad to find him had been the right thing to do, but now, laying in the aftermath of the crazy, hot, amazing sex that only Carter could deliver, she knew this had been the best decision she'd maybe ever made.

And they needed to talk.

"Carter," she said, running her hand along his arm that was still draped over her hips.

He cleared his throat, as if maybe he'd drifted off for a second. "Yeah?"

"I want to stay."

She didn't feel his body tense against her, and for a moment she wondered if he'd heard her. Or if he'd understood her.

"Yeah, you should stay," he finally said.

She shifted to roll and this time he let her.

He wasn't looking at her with love or excitement. He looked resigned.

But he'd said she should stay, so she was going to focus on that.

She put her hand against his cheek. "I want to be here with you."

He nodded, the scruff on his cheek rubbing against her palm. "It's a good idea."

Lacey had to admit that she was surprised at that. "It is?"

He swallowed. "We didn't have a chance to go through the grief period together. I think we both needed that. I think we need some closure on our relationship and feelings for Garrett."

It was strange. She'd just been thinking of Garrett. He hadn't been far from her thoughts since she'd gotten here. Or really at all in the past ten months. But hearing Carter say his name right now, in this moment when she was talking about *them*—her and Carter—was jarring.

"You think so?"

"We didn't even talk after he died, Lace," Carter said gently. "I didn't get to hold you. We didn't cry together. We didn't have that chance to get to where we were sharing stories and memories and smiling about what we had with him. That's an important place to get to in the grief process."

She had to admit he had a point. She'd talked to Garrett's sister, mom and dad. She'd talked to her own sister and parents and a few friends. She'd even met with a counselor a couple of times over all of the mixed-up feelings. But no one knew Garrett like Carter and no one was mourning Garrett like she was except for this man.

"You think that I'm here because I want to grieve?" she asked.

He looked her directly in the eye. "I think that you need to grieve if you want to move on."

She didn't dare ask if he meant moving on with *him* or just in general. But he did seem genuinely concerned about her and that warmed her.

"You reminded me too much of him," she said. "And seeing you at the funeral stirred up so many feelings—like guilt. And anger."

"Because I left."

She nodded. "Yes. And it took Garrett *dying* to bring you back." She felt a tiny surge of anger even in that moment.

He pulled a breath in through his nose. "I was an asshole. But it's important that you remember that, Lacey. I don't really know how to have positive, long-lasting, be-there-through-it-all relationships."

She realized he was warning her off and fortunately she'd expected it. Or that would have hurt.

Well, Carter was going to quickly realize that he knew a lot about her…but he didn't know everything. Like how tenacious she could be, especially when it came to the happiness of people she cared about.

She'd been her grandfather's advocate for years— with others, including her own family, healthcare providers, and insurance companies, and even with him. When he didn't think he needed help or when he refused to do what *he* needed to do to take care of himself. She knew how to fight for what was right. Helping run a nonprofit for mental health meant she knew a lot about people throwing up obstacles to avoid doing something difficult, even if it was right. Being with Carter in every way, for the long term, was what would make *him* happy, and she would fight tooth and nail for that. But even more, it was what would make *her* happy, and she would *never* stop fighting for that.

"Well, it just so happens, I know *a lot* about being there no matter what," she said, running her hand over his chest. "I'll teach you."

She saw his jaw tighten and him swallow hard again. But his tone was gentle when he said, "You're giving me your body. And I'm too damned weak to say no to that. So I'm going to grab on and absolutely exhaust both of us, fucking you in every single way I can think of. Twice. But that's free now."

Lacey frowned. "What do you mean?"

"I can't take what isn't free."

She pulled back to look at him better. "What's not free to be taken?"

"Your heart, Lace."

"But..." She shook her head, trying to gather her thoughts. "I'll always love Garrett, of course. But a heart has an infinite ability to love, Carter. And I've always loved you. That's not new."

He didn't say anything for a few seconds. When he finally did, she wished he hadn't.

"But I can't love you fully, Lacey."

She flinched. "Yes, you can."

"I love you but...Garrett helped make it work. And I made it work for him. That's why I didn't think he would be good enough for you long term. He would have committed, but he wasn't good at all of it either. But with you two, I was the best I'll ever be."

He paused then, as if he was letting his words sink in.

And they did.

"You think you need Garrett? You think that two halves of a whole man thing is real?"

Carter ran his hand over her hip. "I can't be like Garrett. I can't do things the way he did. Yeah, that was real."

She frowned. She'd loved them all together. She wanted, needed, to be *loved*. Like she'd felt she was when she was with Carter and Garrett together. Was it possible that they *did* need Garrett to be everything they could be? To be complete?

And if so, that was over. Forever.

A cold chill went through her and she shivered.

"Here, cover up."

He started to pull the sheet up over her but she pushed away. "No. Um. Maybe I'll just take a shower."

Carter let her go. "Okay. Everything you need should be in there."

She just needed a minute by herself. She needed to think through everything. And figure out what she wanted to do next.

Then she needed to figure out what Carter wanted to do next.

She padded naked to the bathroom door. It didn't even occur to her to be self-conscious until she turned back.

He was watching her with a renewed heat in his eyes that she felt from clear across the room. Was it possible to have that heat and *only* that heat?

"Do you have a guest room?" she asked.

He looked surprised for a moment, then he nodded. "Yes."

"I can stay in there," she offered.

He looked almost angry but he gave her a hot look and said, "You agreed that your body is mine."

Damn. For a second she couldn't breathe. So she nodded.

"And that I could have it anywhere, anytime I wanted," he added.

She was getting hot and wet all over again. She nodded.

"And I want you in this bed. Every night you're here, and some days too. Got it?"

She nodded, wondering if she looked like an idiot.

"So go shower. But do not get yourself off in there."

Her eyes widened. "I wouldn't—"

"Well, I certainly hope you do sometimes," he said. "I've surely pictured it. While I'm getting myself off."

She moaned as that image came fully to mind.

"But you're not going to do that now. Shower. Breathe. And then get back in here. Don't bother with any clothes."

If he hadn't added the "breathe" she wouldn't have realized that he understood she needed some time and space. Maybe he did too.

She nodded *again.* "Okay."

Sleeping in his arms was a temptation she couldn't pass up. More sex before sleeping in his arms was something her body was already preparing for, seemingly.

She slipped into the bathroom, closed the door and leaned against it, doing the most important thing on his list of commands.

She just breathed.

HE WAS SO FUCKED.

Carter's smile died the moment Lacey shut the bathroom door.

What the *hell* was wrong with him?

He'd hurt her. The last person on earth he wanted to cause pain. The person he'd been specifically avoiding so he *wouldn't* cause her pain.

At least he'd been honest when he told her that he was no good at the long-term, unconditional-relationship thing.

But he was right about him and Garrett being good for Lacey *together*. Hell, Garrett had agreed with him. Sure, they'd yelled it at each other on Garrett's driveway after almost sharing Lacey sexually…which was kind of fucked up…but Garrett had agreed.

Then he'd fucking *proposed* to her a week later.

He'd texted Carter to tell him.

It didn't matter now, though, did it?

Garrett was gone, Lacey was here wanting him, and he could finally have her all to himself forever.

And feel like a complete dickhead forever.

He'd wanted them to break-up. He'd wanted her to realize

that she didn't want *just* Garrett. That he wasn't enough by himself.

He'd wanted her to come to Carter and want him back.

And now here she was.

Carter dug the heels of his hands into his eyes.

Dammit.

He couldn't apologize and talk it out and get blisteringly drunk with a ghost.

He felt her before he heard her. Lacey moved back into the room and it felt as if all of the air molecules shifted around him.

But he didn't move his hands. He wasn't sure he could look at her yet. Not without wanting everything and saying to hell with it even though he knew she deserved better.

The mattress dipped as she sat down and the next thing he felt was her curling against his side, tucking her leg between his and resting her hand on his stomach.

She was naked and smelling fresh and clean. Which only made him want to mark her again with his scent and the scent of them together.

Carter was glad he hadn't taken his pants all the way off and that he'd at least tucked himself back in, even if he hadn't zipped up.

He wanted her again. Still. But they had to cool this off.

He needed to know what she was here for. She said she'd come because it was her birthday. She was sad, lonely. She'd missed him.

That all made sense. But she'd also done more than hint that she wanted more than sex. That Garrett would have been okay with it, would have chosen it.

That might be true.

But Garrett didn't know shit about relationships either.

Garrett had wanted things to stay as they had been. Looking back, Carter realized that. He knew now, in retrospect, that's what Lacey's birthday had been about. Garrett giving Carter the one thing with Lacey that he didn't have. The bedroom.

Garrett *had* realized Carter loved her. What he hadn't known was that *Carter* wouldn't share her.

Because Garrett wasn't planning to give her up. He'd thought they could share her. Long-term. He'd thought Carter would move back to Baton Rouge and they'd live in some kind of throuple arrangement or something.

And if Carter had gone along with it, Garrett never would have proposed. They probably would have lived forever the way they had been—three best friends, spending all their free time together, laughing, loving...and fucking. Garrett had been willing to share it all with Carter.

And now what? Carter wanted to yell at Garrett. *What the fuck am I supposed to do now?*

He shifted, sliding his arm under and around Lacey and pulling her closer. She put her cheek against his chest.

"Tell me about that night," he said.

She didn't need clarification. He wasn't asking about the night they'd been together.

"It was just a normal night," she said. "It was a Thursday. I made pasta and was watching shows I'd recorded on my DVR in my pajamas." She paused, then laughed softly. "Isn't it stupid that I remember the pasta? Rotini with carbonara sauce."

Carter tightened his arm around her. She sounded okay and he so desperately wanted to believe she was.

"Anyway, things were just normal. Or I thought they were. I went to bed. I do remember having trouble falling asleep, but I was asleep when they knocked on the door."

God. Carter kept his eyes shut, but ran his hand up and down her back.

"It was also a pretty typical call. They were called to a possible burglary and followed the suspect down an alley and he pulled a gun and Garrett advanced, hoping to talk him down and...he didn't."

"He didn't have a vest on?" Carter asked. That had always bothered him. But he regretted asking it after the words came.

Lacey didn't tighten up or pull away though. "The bullet got him in the neck."

Lacey's voice was thick and Carter hated himself for starting this conversation.

"Never mind, Lace."

"No."

He felt her move and he opened his eyes. She had her hands on his chest, her chin on top of them. "You don't have to," he said quietly.

"No one ever asks me about stuff like that," she said. "Everyone treats me like I'm breakable. I don't want it to be like that with you. I'm *not* breakable."

He looked into her eyes, the big brown eyes that he'd drowned in multiple times. But he saw something there now that he hadn't before—or he hadn't looked for before.

Strength.

He had to admit the words that came to mind when he thought of Lacey were sweet and warm and kind and loving. Soft words. Words that were the opposite of things he thought of himself. Words that took the edge off of him.

But there was more there. Now there was a determination he had never seen, along with a sadness that he knew was new and permanent. And it made him want to make her smile and laugh, to see those eyes sparkle with mischief and passion and joy.

Things he'd never thought of before. That wasn't his deal. That had been Garrett's job.

But now…

"Okay, tough girl," he said, rolling to face her and reaching for the sheet to pull up over her nakedness. He was trying to be a good guy, but he was no saint. "Tell me everything you want me to know."

Her expression softened. She wet her lips and took a breath. "The bullet hit his jugular. He died quickly. I've been grateful for that in some ways but in others… I'm pissed I didn't get to say goodbye or have even five minutes of clinging to some hope that it would be okay. And then I think that would have been a lot worse. And not fair to him, of course. I would have never wanted him to suffer. But it was just so sudden. It was over before I even knew anything had happened. It took days for it to really sink in."

Carter had expected his chest to tighten and his gut to churn, hearing about that night. Instead, strangely, he felt like something had lifted from his chest.

He didn't like the story, but he loved no longer wondering.

"Did you help with the funeral?"

Garrett had family and he had the force. With him and Lacey not married, it was possible they'd left her out of things.

"His mom asked me to pick some music," Lacey said. "And I chose the poem you read."

Carter nodded. "I figured."

Garrett's mother had actually been the one to ask him to read something at the service and he'd been touched and grateful to be included. They'd said they had a special poem already chosen and he'd been fine with that. They'd emailed it to him ahead of time and as soon as he'd read it, somehow he'd known Lacey had picked it.

"You did?" she looked surprised, but pleased.

"Yeah. There was something about it."

She smiled. "I'm glad you knew."

"I wish I had known for sure. I wish we could have talked," he said, deciding that he wanted her full honesty, so he had to give her his. "It made me feel more connected to you. Like we were sharing that day. But I wanted to hold you. Your hand at least. I wanted to hug you and comfort you and...have you comfort me."

Her smiled faded but she nodded. "I'm sorry about that."

"So, I have a proposition." He pulled her closer before he said the rest, wanting her to know that he wasn't pushing her away.

"Okay."

"I think we need to make this visit about him. And healing.

Getting past some of this and figuring out how we feel now, what we really want."

Lacey frowned lightly. "That doesn't sound like the Carter I know."

Yeah, this was all very *emotional*. Something he didn't typically do. "I know."

"I think you're saying what you think you're supposed to say," she told him.

"And I think maybe you're here for the same reason you *didn't* talk to me at the funeral," he replied.

She pulled back. "What do you mean?"

"You didn't talk to me at the funeral because I reminded you too much of him. And I think you're here now because I remind you of him. You've gotten past some of the initial pain but now you're missing him."

She pulled back even farther, putting space between them. "Of course I miss him."

"I can't be a stand-in for him, Lacey." And that was the absolute truth. Even if he wanted to be.

"I'm not trying to replace him."

"You're trying to fill a hole in your heart."

"Yes. With love. With the only other man I've ever felt that for. With the only other man who has felt that for me. With the man who left that hole in my heart a year ago."

He flinched a little with that. And she noticed.

"Yeah. You left a hole before he did. Now I have *two* big gaping holes in my heart. And I can only fill one of them."

She was breathing a little fast now and her eyes were definitely sparkling. In fact, they were flashing.

He liked seeing this. He liked this a lot better than sad. He also loved knowing that she loved him and he loved that it had mattered when he left. He hadn't realized he had a sadistic tendency, but yeah, it was nice to know he'd been missed.

However, he couldn't let her get too overboard here with the

L word. She was absolutely as close as he'd ever come, but that didn't mean that he'd be any good at it.

"Lace, I told you…so much of what I felt for you was about Garrett and—"

"Bullshit."

He stared at her. "What?"

"I thought about it in the shower and I don't believe you," she said. "When we were together it was amazing and yes, of course, that was about Garrett too, and no, we won't ever be able to replicate that. I wouldn't want to. But you and I had a connection that had nothing to do with Garrett and I felt it again here tonight. It will be different without him. But it will still be good, Carter. Really, really good."

The earnestness in her voice and eyes was almost his undoing.

That and the fact that he *really* liked what she was saying and *really* wanted to believe it all.

"I *knew* we shouldn't have had sex right away tonight," he muttered, though he knew she heard him.

One corner of her mouth curled. "But we did. And now we both know the truth. We have something amazing." She sat up partially, bracing one hand on the mattress, locking her elbow and holding the sheet against her breasts with the other. She looked down at him with utter seriousness. "I lost one love, Carter. I'm not losing the other. You're here. We're *both* still here. Breathing, living. I'm not letting go of this chance for happiness. I'm not going to let *you* let go of it either."

His mind knew he should protest. He knew that he should push her away, insist he was no good for her, tell her that her happiness was somewhere else. But he couldn't. Because he'd been feeling the same regret, the same loss, for the past year.

But with that realization came the fear.

His father always wanted to be with his wives too. He truly thought he loved them. He fell for them hook, line and sinker and he got them married, bound to him, as quickly as possible. And he made it hell on them to leave.

They all did, eventually. But it was a battle. Matt Shaw used everything he had to keep them with him—begging, pleading, threatening, lying, cutting off their money, tangling them up in legal messes, even stooping to ridiculousness like hiding their car keys, or hiding their *car*. He went to such lengths that it was humiliating for all of them. Carter less so, now that he was out on his own and away from the crazy, but Matt was still his father and everyone in town knew all about the drama. Every fucking time.

Why these women kept signing up for Matt's particular brand of hell, Carter didn't know. Apparently Matt was as passionate and over the top when falling in love as he was in trying to keep his marriages together when they fell apart. He swept them off their feet. And married them as fast as he could. The only thing he didn't do, obviously, was give them a real reason to stay.

Carter felt a similar type of desperation when he thought about Lacey.

The idea of being able to have her, all to himself, forever, made him feel a little crazy for sure. And the idea of having her and then losing her…yep, that could absolutely send him over the edge.

Fuck.

He made himself say, "I want you to be happy, Lacey. I do. I just don't know—"

She put a finger over his lips. "Just let me stay. For a while. Let's see how it goes. I took a leave of absence from work. I didn't take much time off after the funeral—I needed to drown myself in work then—so they were happy to give me time off now. Let me just stay and be with you. We can…take it a little at a time."

And with those big brown eyes on his, her body smelling like his soap, wrapped only in his sheet, in his bed, Carter said the only thing possible. "Okay. Stay."

———

They slept after that.

Lacey was amazed when she awoke nearly nine hours later. She hadn't slept that well, or that long, since before the night Garrett had been shot. She'd been honest when she'd said that she'd had trouble falling asleep that night.

She rolled to her back and stretched.

She was a little sore and that made her smile. She hadn't had a reason to be that kind of sore in a long time either.

Without looking, she knew that Carter wasn't in bed with her.

This was the second time she'd gone to sleep with him and awakened without him, and she didn't like it. But in all fairness, she'd shown up out of the blue last night. It was possible he had plans. This was his house, his town, his *life*. She was interrupting.

But she didn't think he minded.

There had been a lot of emotions swirling last night. That was part of the reason they'd fallen asleep rather than getting even sorer.

But they'd fallen asleep *together*. Wrapped around one another. All night.

That was the stuff she needed, what she'd hoped for in coming here.

Lacey stretched, unable to stop smiling.

Carter was still processing it all, and considering she'd been thinking about this trip for almost two weeks before making it while he'd only known how she felt and what she wanted for a few hours, she knew she had to give him time.

He thought they were going to make this trip about Garrett and healing and dealing.

That was fine. Smart. Probably something they needed.

But she was here for *Carter*. She was done being sad and moving through her life numb and only half there. She wanted her life back. She wanted love and laughter and passion and friendship and there was only one man left on the planet who could give her those things.

And she was waking up in his bed.

That was a very good start.

Lacey got up, grinning at the torn pair of blue panties on Carter's floor. That was a perfect place to leave them too, she figured. She had a suitcase in the car, but since all she'd worn inside was the lingerie and trench coat and heels, she padded to his closet. She could have rifled through his drawers for a t-shirt but there had been something about that dress shirt he'd worn last night that made her heart thump. He'd been dressed the same way the first time she'd met him. He'd been in dark-gray dress pants and white button-down shirt with the sleeves rolled up. If he'd worn a tie to the wedding, he'd already shed it by the time he and Garrett approached her at the reception.

Last night he'd looked the same. Black pants, dark-blue dress shirt, sleeves rolled up, no tie. Of course, last night he'd also worn something even sexier—an in-charge but calm attitude when he'd come into his neighbor's house, supposedly to deal with a burglar, or a mistress, or whatever they'd all thought she was.

She'd been embarrassed about the whole thing—getting the wrong house, almost being arrested—but she'd been hot for the commanding cop who'd come through the door, that was for sure.

In the past, Carter had come to Baton Rouge to hang out. He wore jeans, T-shirts and ball caps. He'd dress up a little with a knit shirt and nicer jeans if they went out, but he didn't give a lot of time or energy to his appearance. He kept his hair short and a seemingly perpetual scruff on his face.

He was hot, sexy, gorgeous. But it all seemed second nature.

He worked out because he liked it and needed it for his job. His sexiness came, not from his hair or clothes, but from the way he moved and the confidence and intensity that was just a part of him.

Lacey pulled a white shirt from a hanger and slipped into it. She loved the smell of it around her and how it seemed to engulf her body—like Carter did.

In the bathroom, she washed her face and ran Carter's comb through her hair, then headed downstairs.

If he wasn't here, she certainly hoped he'd left the coffee pot on. She knew he drank it, by the gallons. Of course, he drank it straight-up black so she also hoped he had cream or at least milk. She couldn't take how he and Garrett did coffee. It wasn't supposed to eat a hole in your gut.

The kitchen was empty but there was a note on the counter.

Even before she read it, she was warmed by it.

Out for a run. Be back soon. Make yourself at home.

Oh, she intended to, she thought, smiling.

In fact…

Twenty minutes later, when Carter came in through the back door, Lacey had just added the final pancakes to the stack on the plate and had reached into the cupboard above for the syrup. It had taken a little bit to find all of the ingredients, but he'd had everything she needed.

She turned to greet him but her words dried up on her lips.

Carter was looking at her as if she'd just punched him in the gut. He was also shirtless, sweaty, breathing hard. "Jesus," he muttered, his gaze sweeping over her.

Everything in her clenched tight and hard with just that look.

"What?" she managed to ask.

"Do you realize when you reach up like that, your sweet ass is on display?" he asked roughly.

She hadn't really thought about it actually. But now she was very aware of her ass—and lots of other things.

She cleared her throat. "I made breakfast."

"A hot girl I want more than anything, dressed in my shirt, clearly naked underneath and smelling like pancakes," Carter said, moving around the corner of the island. "I don't need any breakfast."

Her gaze traveled down his neck to his chest, over his pecs and down his abs. Her tongue tingled. "You shouldn't run around town looking like that," she told him. "It's not fair to the other men. Or the women trying to get anything done."

The corner of his mouth curled slightly. "I like knowing I can get you all hot and bothered as easy as you do it to me."

He stopped right in front of her.

"You can. You do," she said, her voice husky.

"Take the shirt off."

She had not expected things to go down like this. She'd honestly made him breakfast thinking they would talk and have coffee and find their way back to the fun, easygoing friendship they'd had before.

She'd always been attracted to him, had fantasized about sex with him, felt the heat between them. But she valued the friendship too.

Of course, they'd never been alone together. Last night, when they'd come through his front door, had been the first time they'd truly been alone. There had been times when it had been just the two of them for a few minutes, but Garrett had always been there, or in just the next room. In fact, as she thought about it, there had been a few times that Garrett had been running late getting out of work and making it to dinner on time but she and Carter had been left waiting in a restaurant or, if at home, with a group of friends. Never really alone.

She frowned as that realization caught up to her.

"Did Garrett keep us from being alone or was that you?" she asked.

It was clear that her question seemed out of the blue to Carter. He stopped with his hand partway to her hair and frowned. "What?"

"You and I have never been alone until last night. Even if Garrett wasn't there, we were in public or with other people. Did he do that or did you?"

Carter's hand dropped back to his side. "Maybe it was just a coincidence."

She didn't buy it. "Or maybe one of you worked it out that way."

Carter looked into her eyes. "Why do you think we would do that?"

"Because all three of us knew that there was something between you and me from the very beginning. Maybe one of you was afraid of what would happen if we were alone for even a few minutes."

He moved in closer, his eyes darkening. "And what would have happened?"

"We would have kissed. Probably more."

"In just a few minutes?"

She shrugged. "Yes."

"Really." But he wasn't asking. He knew the answer.

"So who kept us apart?"

He didn't even blink. "We both did."

She wasn't surprised, she realized. "You talked about it."

"That I wanted you from the minute I saw you? Yes. Though we didn't really need to talk about it. He knew me well enough to know."

"Might have had something to do with you saying 'damn, I'd like to put her up against the nearest wall' to him when you both noticed me."

One eyebrow arched. "He told you that?"

"He did."

"Do you know that he told me about the two of you in the bedroom?" Carter asked.

Lacey had to admit she was surprised at that. "What about us?"

"That you love it from behind. That you're a dirty talker. That you're the best blow job he's ever had. That country music makes you horny— especially Chase Rice and Kip Moore. That—"

"Okay." She wasn't sure if she should laugh or shake her head or shove him back or pull him closer. "And you clearly never told him to stop."

"I should have," he said. "But I liked hearing it. It made my fantasies even better. When I was jerking off and thinking of you, I could imagine your mouth around my cock and you saying beautiful, filthy things, and then begging me to take you from behind."

He'd continued moving closer as he spoke and Lacey felt her whole body flush.

He was so… *God*.

"With my mouth around your cock it would have been hard to say filthy things."

He gave her a lethal half grin. "Somehow it all worked in my mind."

"Garrett didn't mind us thinking about each other sexually," she said, as that realization hit her.

Carter braced his hands on the counter on either side of her hips. "Nope. He admitted it when he told me the plan for your birthday. But I suspected it before that. I think he wanted to share you before that but wanted to ease you into it."

Her breath hitched with him this close, half naked, big and hot and nearly on top of her.

"He should have brought it up before I fell for you though," Carter said. "I would have said yes early on. Before I realized I could never share you with anyone else."

She gave a little moan. It was that combination of sweet and hot again. Knowing he had fallen for her made her warm all over, but the idea that she could have had him in her bed months ago made hot yearning spill through her belly and lower.

"How early on?"

She was really asking when he'd realized that he felt more for her than just attraction.

She saw in his eyes he understood that.

"Three months," he answered after a long pause.

Lacey's eyebrows rose. "That was the window?"

"Yep. After that, it was so much more."

Holy…

"And Garrett knew that?" she asked.

"No. Not for a long time."

"So then why did he never leave us alone together?" she asked, breathless.

"That was me."

"Why?" She bit her bottom lip. She shouldn't ask that, shouldn't even wonder. But God she did.

"Because if I'd had you alone for five minutes, I would have been buried balls deep. And then I would have made you choose between us."

She felt her nipples pull tight and everything deep pulse even as the seriousness of his words sank in.

"He wanted to share. You didn't. And the night of my birthday, that's how it turned out," she finally said.

"Yeah. But I didn't make *you* choose. I told *him* to walk away. And he didn't."

"He thought you would come around."

Carter shook his head. "He proposed. I wouldn't have come around after that. He was finally staking a real claim."

Lacey had no idea what she was feeling now. "You said that you called him and wanted to talk things out."

"I was getting damned sick of going without you. Both of you. I was drunk and decided that if I had to share you, at least I would have part of you." He paused. "It wouldn't have worked. It would have come between him and me and we all would have broken up with lots of hurt feelings. But it would have been spectacularly dirty and hot and fun for a short time."

She blew out a breath. "I don't know what to say." She was overwhelmed.

And now he could have her, not share, be everything. This could work.

This had to work.

"So Garrett knew you wanted me and that you didn't want to share and that if we'd ever been alone together something would have happened, but we've been in here, alone, for more than five minutes," she pointed out, "and you're not balls deep."

She'd expected him to hesitate or to be surprised for three seconds.

He wasn't.

"Turn around," he growled.

"I want to see you."

"I'm all sweaty, and not in the nice, sexy way," he said. "Turn around."

She shivered and did as he asked.

He ran a hand up the back of her thigh to her bare ass and stroked over her cheek before pushing the shirt to her lower back.

She pressed into his hand. "I don't mind sweaty."

"But you *love* it from behind. Deep and hard. Or so I've heard."

She moaned. She did. So, so much. And it didn't seem to bother Carter that what he knew about her had come from his best friend who had been sleeping with her. For some reason, that was kind of hot too. Confusing. But hot.

"Brace yourself, darlin'."

CHAPTER
SIX

LACEY GRABBED the edge of the counter and widened her stance. She heard the swish of his running shorts and then felt his hot, hard cock against her butt.

"You are a fucking dream come true," he murmured, running his hand around her stomach and then down.

She whimpered as he circled her clit before sliding lower.

"So wet," he praised. "So needy."

"God, Carter." Her head dropped forward as he thrust a finger deep, stroking three times before adding a second.

"What do you need, Lace?"

"You."

"Tell me. I want to hear specifics."

"Your cock, hard and deep." She gasped as he stroked a fingertip over her G-spot.

He grabbed her leg and lifted her thigh, opening her. "Bend over."

She leaned into the counter and immediately felt the head of his cock at her entrance. He thrust, sinking into her in one stroke.

She heard him draw a ragged breath. "Balls deep," he said gruffly.

She smiled and wiggled against him. "About time."

He chuckled softly. "So that's how it is."

"Just for future reference, if we're alone together for five minutes, this is what I expect."

"Dream come true," he repeated.

Then he began moving.

He thrust deep, hard and fast. Just the way she liked it.

She was climbing quickly, but when he said, "Fingers on your clit, Lace," she almost shot to the edge. She knew that touching herself would make short work of the pending orgasm and she hesitated. She wanted to prolong this.

But Carter moved his hand to her breast and pinched her nipple. "Clit. Now. I want you to come hard."

She couldn't resist. She was on fire and she needed the release suddenly like she needed her next breath. She touched herself as he continued to pound into her and tug on her nipple and it wasn't even a full minute later that she was shooting over the summit.

"Fuck yes." He grabbed both of her hips, pulling her back hard against him as he powered into her and he came a few strokes later.

He pulled out of her almost immediately, yanking his shorts back into place. But he took her hand when he started across the tile.

"Carter. Pancakes," she said as she followed him.

"Lacey. Shower."

She smiled. She also loved shower sex. But Garrett had probably told Carter that.

She was determined to find something that she'd never done with Garrett.

After her shower with Carter.

An hour later, they were finally both dressed, her in a T-shirt and capris with sandals, Carter in jeans and a tee. And they had their hands off of each other. They were back in the kitchen and she was preparing to heat up the pancakes.

Carter had a little frown on his face though.

"What's wrong?" she asked, plate in hand.

"Nothing."

"Carter. What's wrong?"

He sighed. "It's stupid."

She set the plate down. "What is it? You don't like pancakes?"

"Sure. They're great."

"But?"

"Garrett loved pancakes."

She looked at the plate. "Yeah, he did." They were his favorite thing, in fact.

"I'll bet you made them for him a lot."

She made amazing pancakes. She pushed her hand through her hair. "Yeah."

They were both quiet for a moment.

Finally Carter said, "Told you it was stupid."

Lacey looked up. There was something in his voice, in this whole thing that seemed so strange. "You never seemed jealous of him," she said.

He shook his head. "I was jealous as hell, Lacey."

She shouldn't like that he was jealous. But apparently she wasn't such a sweetheart after all.

She picked up the plate of pancakes and stepped to the trashcan. She pressed the lever with her foot and tossed them in. Turning to face him with the empty plate, she said, "We should go out for breakfast."

He looked from her to the trashcan and back. And he smiled.

Her heart kicked in her chest and she became determined to make *that* happen a lot as well.

"Leave the house?" he teased. "That will make it hard to keep you naked."

Yeah, it would, and suddenly she realized that she needed to be *less* naked with Carter. His words from the night before came back to her. *Sex I can do. As much as you want, for as long as you need it.*

She wanted more from him than that. He either didn't believe that or was ignoring it or was hoping to fry her brain cells with hot sex so she wouldn't remember it, but she did. And being *not* naked for a while was the best bet for showing him.

"Yes, leave the house. Go out. Do something. Show me Bad." A thought occurred to her. "Garrett grew up here too. Show me around, where you guys used to hang out."

Something flickered in his eyes, but he nodded. "Yeah, okay, let's do that."

There was a thump at the back door as she turned to put the plate in the sink.

Lacey looked over. "Um, Carter, there's a cat thumping his head against your back door."

Carter sighed. "I know."

He crossed to the door and swung it open for the black-and-gray tabby that strolled in as if it owned the place.

"You have a cat?" That so did not fit her image of him for some reason.

"More like the cat has me," he said wryly, crossing to one of the cupboards and pulling out a bag of cat food. "He's a stray that just showed up one night."

She couldn't help but smile at the way the cat completely ignored her, but followed Carter, circling his ankles and rubbing against his calves.

Smart cat.

"And you fed him," she guessed.

"Had to. He was obviously starving." Carter filled a bowl with water and then squatted by the cat with the water and another bowl for food.

"You let him into the kitchen to feed him?" She leaned against the counter and crossed her arms, watching Carter rub a thumb between the cat's ears and stroke over his back as the cat arched and purred.

Very smart cat.

"It was cold that night," he said without looking up.

Lacey's smile grew. This was Bad, Louisiana. It didn't get that cold. "How long ago was that?" Considering they were now in August, it hadn't been even slightly cold for months.

"A while." Carter filled the bowl and the cat dug in. But not like a starving animal. More like a well-cared-for pet that knew it was time for breakfast.

Carter stretched to his feet. "You ready?"

"You're not going to wait and let him back out?" she asked, already knowing the answer.

"He'll, um—" Carter cleared his throat, looking at the cat instead of her. "He'll probably just curl up somewhere 'til we get back."

Lacey loved this. He was a softie. For a stray cat. She wanted to hug him and tell him how sweet it was but she knew that would not be welcomed. "He won't need to go out to go to the bathroom?"

She'd put good money on the fact that Carter Shaw, big bad tough cop, had a litter box somewhere in this house that he cleaned for this "stray" cat. She wouldn't even be surprised to find a special pillow somewhere.

"He'll be okay," Carter said simply.

Lacey gave a soft laugh and held out her hand. "Okay, then, let's go."

He seemed relieved she'd dropped it as they headed out front to his truck, but once he was behind the wheel and backing out of the drive, she couldn't help but say, "Being sweet with that stray cat is so getting you laid later."

Carter choked on a laugh. "I didn't realize there was any question about me getting laid later."

She laughed as well. "Well, okay. Good point. But I like your cat."

"He makes a huge mess when he's eating, gets cat hair on everything and knocks the bathroom trashcan over looking for dental floss to play with."

She loved the tone of affection in his voice. "I bet he likes to sit on your lap."

"He insists on drinking water and iced tea out of my glass."

She grinned. "He likes iced tea?"

"He's a big mooch."

But he said it with a smile and Lacey's heart swelled a little.

They drove through a quiet neighborhood of quaint well-kept houses and came out on the main street. The downtown area was just as charming. Okay, maybe quirky was a better word, Lacey realized once she started reading signs.

"The medical clinic is actually called Bad Medicine?" she asked.

Carter nodded. "And the hair salon is Bad Hair Day? And the newspaper is Bad News. And so on. We think we're pretty hilarious."

Lacey laughed. "You're right."

"It's memorable anyway. The church is Bad Faith Community Church."

"Oh, wow," Lacey said with a little grimace.

"Yeah. And my friend Regan's physical therapy clinic is The Bad Place, which everyone agrees is spot on."

Lacey laughed again. "Bet she sells a ton of t-shirts."

"That she does."

There were a few people out on the sidewalks but the most popular place was clearly the coffee shop, judging by the line coming out of the front door.

Carter pulled up in front of the diner, The Bad Egg.

Lacey pivoted on the seat to look back at the coffee shop. Bad Habit. Perfect. "Why not there?" she asked.

Not that the diner didn't look fine, but the coffee shop was jumping.

"Bad Habit doesn't have eggs," Carter said, opening his door and jumping out.

Lacey was suspicious. She slid off of her seat and slammed her door, meeting him at the front of the truck.

"It has lots of your friends though," she said.

Carter sighed. "Yeah, probably."

"And you don't want to take me over there because you don't want me to meet your friends?" she asked.

"It's just… people are nosy here."

She lifted an eyebrow. She didn't think Carter was embarrassed of her exactly. But there was some reason he didn't want to take her to the coffee shop. "What's going on?"

He met her eyes but seemed to be considering his words.

"Carter, we've been totally honest with each other so far. Let's not change that now, okay?"

"Fine. I don't…take women out in Bad."

"What do you mean?"

"I don't date locally. And if a woman does spend the night here with me, we definitely don't go out together the day after."

She kind of liked that. She was *not* going to ask how many had been with him here in Bad though. She had no right, for one thing. And for another, she was pretty sure the number would make her eyes widen.

"Because you haven't been serious with anyone," she said out loud.

He nodded.

"And if you walked into the coffee shop on a Sunday morning with a woman, they would all know that it *was* something serious."

He nodded again. Though slower this time.

She gave him a smile and turned on her heel, heading across the street.

He was right behind her, clearly anticipating her move. "Lace—"

"Officer Shaw, you can throw me over your shoulder and carry me back to your truck, but I am going to holler. Just so you know."

She knew she was being ballsy. She was assuming a lot. She was gambling. But if the women around here were too stupid to make a big, spectacular play for Carter, that was their problem. She wasn't stupid. And she knew how he felt about her.

She also knew he was stubborn. He was convinced he wasn't good enough for her. She was going to prove to him that she didn't agree.

"Lacey, what—" He grabbed her arm when she didn't stop and pulled her around to face him. Right in the middle of the street. "What do think is going to happen in there?"

"I think that you're going to have to explain to everyone who I am," she said.

"And what am I supposed to say?"

"The truth."

His eyes searched hers. "What truth?"

"That I'm yours."

His pupils dilated at that. "And I'm going to tell them that?"

"I don't know how you're going to word it exactly, but I do think you'll claim me, yes. You won't want anyone thinking I'm just a one-night thing that doesn't even have a last name as far as you know, because you respect me and don't want them thinking that of me. And I'm going to be around for more than one night so that will blow that lie out of the water anyway. And you won't want them to think I'm a free agent, because you won't want anyone else asking me out. And you won't want them to think I'm just a friend from out of town in Bad for a long visit because she'd been through a tough, sad time lately since her fiancé died."

There was a moment of silence between them.

"Why won't I want them to think that last thing?" he finally asked.

His voice was a little rough and she knew she was winning this gamble.

"Because you're going to want to touch me and hold my hand and kiss me and that will all seem inappropriate if our only connection is my dead fiancé."

She saw how he flinched at her words and she grabbed his

hand before he pulled back. "Carter, I'm not Garrett's widow. I was his fiancé but you know there was a lot more going on than that. What's happened—and is going to keep happening—between us is *not* inappropriate."

"What am I supposed to say?" he asked, an angry edge to his voice now. "Garrett was from here. How will it look that I'm hooking up with his ex? How am I supposed to explain all of that?"

She frowned. "Don't explain it at all. It's nobody's business but ours."

It was easy for her to say all of that, but she had to admit that when it came to her friends and family in Baton Rouge, she hadn't really thought through how she would explain what she was doing with Garrett's best friend now.

It looked a little pathetic. Like she was rebounding from his death. Like she was so distraught that she'd run to Carter and was drowning her sorrows in sex with the guy closest to Garrett.

She drew back, dropping Carter's hand. She hated all of those thoughts. Yeah, she could understand why it might *seem* that way, but it wasn't the truth. And the only people that needed to know everything was her and Carter.

A car gave a quick honk to get past them.

Carter grabbed her arm again and pulled her up onto the sidewalk in front of the coffee shop, then gave the car a little wave.

"So, we don't mention Garrett," Carter finally said.

"Right," she said, sounding much surer than she felt. "It's not about Garrett."

Carter looked like he was going to say something more to that. But finally he just nodded. "Okay. It's just you and me."

Lacey took a deep breath. "Okay."

"Brace yourself." He put a hand on her lower back and nudged her toward the coffee shop doorway.

The line was only three people deep by now and Carter steered her in behind the last guy waiting to place an order.

She could feel his tension but he hadn't refused to bring her in here. That was something, she knew.

"Carter!"

They both heard someone call his name at the same time and turned toward the voice.

"Here we go," Carter muttered.

The voice belonged to a big, good-looking guy sitting at a table near the window with a pretty blonde. There were two empty chairs at the table on the side closest to Carter and Lacey.

"Hey guys," Carter called.

"Sit with us." The guy pushed one of the chairs out with his foot.

Carter kept his hand on Lacey's back and started for the table.

"Mornin', Annabelle," Carter said to the blonde.

"Hi," she greeted with a sweet smile. "Didn't know if we'd see you this morning. Jackson said you left the wedding because of a robbery call?"

"You weren't answering your cell after you left," the man said. Clearly he was talking to Carter, but his eyes were on Lacey. "I was wondering how it all went down."

"Jackson, this is Lacey. Lacey, Jackson and Annabelle," Carter said, ignoring Jackson's implied question.

Lacey leaned in and stuck her hand out to Annabelle, who shook it with a soft "hi", and then to Jackson. "It wasn't a robbery," she said. "I just got the wrong house."

Jackson's eyebrows climbed his forehead. "*You* were the call?"

Lacey settled back on her heels and felt Carter's hand on her back again. She was feeling a definitely surge of mischief. "I was trying to surprise Carter, but let myself into the neighbor's instead."

"Let yourself in?" Jackson repeated.

Lacey grinned. "Carter taught me to pick a lock a long time ago."

Carter rolled his eyes. Garrett had been there too, but Carter had been the primary instructor. They'd insisted she learn how to jimmy her car door in case she locked her keys inside or lost them, and in the process, they'd moved on to other locks. And how to hot wire the car.

"A *long* time ago?" Jackson's very curious gaze swung to Carter now.

"Of course, the big surprise was for his neighbor's wife when she saw I was in only a trench coat and lingerie. Just a misunderstanding though."

"Linger—" Jackson's voice suddenly sounded strangled.

"We're going to get coffee," Carter said, turning toward the counter.

"You know what I like," Lacey said. She dropped into the chair Jackson had pushed out.

Carter sighed. "Be good," he said.

But he left her alone with his friends. That meant he trusted her. Or that he didn't care what she told his friends about them. Interesting.

Jackson sat up straighter and leaned in as soon as Carter moved out of earshot. "It's really nice to meet you, Lacey."

"Thanks, Jackson. You and Carter are friends, I take it?" Did her name sound familiar to him at all?

"He's probably my best friend in Bad."

"You grew up together?"

"We did. I was gone for several years after high school, but I'm back now. Annabelle went to school with us too."

Lacey smiled at the other woman. "I'd love to hear stories about Carter from high school."

"I'd love to hear stories about you and Carter," Jackson said.

Ah, so no her name wasn't familiar. Huh. Carter had *never* mentioned her? Not even in regards to how he spent his weekends in Baton Rouge?

"Jackson," Annabelle admonished. She smiled at Lacey. "Sorry."

Lacey shrugged. "What do you want to know?"

"How did you meet?"

Nope, Carter had never mentioned her.

"At a wedding reception."

"How long ago?"

"Two years."

Jackson frowned. "You've been dating him for *two years*?"

Lacey shook her head. "We've known each other that long. Been friends. We just started dating last night." She supposed that was true. They hadn't dated up to that point but now they were more than friends, more than a weekend fling. She intended to keep doing what they were doing. She supposed they could call it dating.

"Last night?" Annabelle said. "That's why you came to Bad? To tell him you wanted to be more than friends?" It was clear the other woman thought that was kind of romantic.

Romantic. Exactly. Not a fling. Not a I'm-too-sad-to-be-alone-on-my-birthday hook up. It was *romantic* that she was here.

"Yes," Lacey said with a big smile.

"And what did Carter say?" Jackson asked.

"What did I say about what?" Carter set two cups of coffee on the table and slid the other chair out.

Jackson sat back and slipped his arm over the back of Annabelle's chair, the picture of nonchalance. "About Lacey showing up and claiming to be in love with you?"

Carter sipped his coffee and Lacey was sure she was the only one who noticed the way his opposite hand twitched.

After he'd swallowed, he said, "I told her to take her clothes off."

Lacey felt a rush of heat and wasn't sure if it was desire or embarrassment.

But she'd started this.

Annabelle coughed. Jackson shifted on his seat. Lacey gathered her bravado, turned toward Carter and said, "Hence our need for so much coffee this morning."

Carter's left eye twitched now.

Perfect.

"Hey guys."

They were interrupted again. This time by a tall, slender guy who everyone automatically smiled at when they looked up.

"Nolan!" Annabelle stood up and leaned across Jackson to give the man a hug.

"Hey AJ," he said, clearly fond of the other woman.

He shook Jackson's hand. "Good to see you, man."

"You too. What are you doing here?"

Nolan also shook Carter's hand. "Shaw."

"Winters," Carter said, clasping the man's hand.

He was blond, his hair longer, a little shaggier than Carter's, but clean-shaven. His green eyes sparkled, and it seemed like he couldn't stop smiling.

"I didn't know you were in town," Carter said.

"Just got in this morning. More research for my book." He pulled up a chair from another table and positioned it at the end of the table with Jackson to his left and Lacey to his right.

"You're sticking around until the ceremony?" Jackson said. "That's another three weeks."

"Yeah, I want to hang out, talk to some people, and I want to cover Coach's ceremony for sure."

"Coach Karr is getting an award?" Lacey asked. Garrett and Carter had both talked fondly of their old high school football coach. He was a father figure to many of the boys who had played for him, and both Garrett and Carter had stayed in touch with him. He'd sent a card after Garrett's death and had made her cry even though she'd never met the man.

"They're renaming the football field after him," Carter said.

"Oh, that's so nice."

"You know Coach Karr?" Jackson asked.

"No, I've just heard a lot about him from Garrett and Carter," Lacey said.

And immediately realized that she'd just spilled the secret.

Carter sighed. Jackson sat up straighter. Annabelle frowned and Nolan looked around the table as if trying to figure out what was going on.

"What's your book about?" she asked Nolan, hoping they could just blow past the whole Garrett thing.

"Garrett Dunn?" Jackson asked. Definitely not blowing past it.

"Yes." Lacey glanced at Carter to find Annabelle reaching for his hand, worry in her eyes.

"You okay?" Annabelle asked him.

Lacey frowned. "Why wouldn't he be okay talking about Garrett?"

"Lace—" Carter said warningly. He didn't finish the statement but he shook his head.

"Garrett was Carter's best friend," Annabelle said. "I assume you know he passed away?"

Lacey stared at her. "Of course I know that." But clearly Carter had never mentioned his weekends with her and Garrett. "Carter spent a lot of time with him in Baton Rouge," Lacey said, gauging their reactions.

"Yes. Garrett didn't get home to Bad much," Annabelle said.

Lacey thought about that. Annabelle was right and it probably seemed strange that Garrett hadn't come home more often. Carter always came to Baton Rouge while Garrett rarely made the trip to Bad. Occasionally he would come back here for a weekend—like Homecoming—but in the time she'd known him, he'd made maybe three trips to Bad. His parents had moved to Baton Rouge after his younger sister graduated from high school. The only things left for him in his hometown were old friends, and the one who mattered most had made the trip to his city on a regular basis.

Lacey had never come along. It had been his chance to catch up with old friends, visit Coach and relive some glory days, so she'd stayed in the city and worked or made it a girls' weekend. Truthfully, since meeting Garrett and Carter, she'd drifted away from a lot of her girlfriends, finding she'd rather spend time with the two guys in her life. So those weekends were good for long lunches and spa days and shopping with her sister and friends. It had never bothered her to not come to Bad.

"I know that he didn't come back here much. He was busy on the weekends in the city," Lacey said.

Not that they'd dated the entire time he'd been living in Baton Rouge of course. Garrett and Carter had both lived in Baton Rouge for years before they'd met Lacey. They'd gotten criminal justice degrees and then joined the police force. They'd been partners for almost five years. Carter had only moved back to Bad a year and a half ago—about six months into her relationship with Garrett.

It had been hard on Garrett having his closest friend leave and starting over with a new partner. But he'd had Lacey. They'd been almost inseparable after Carter moved back home.

Then Jackson asked, "How did you know Garrett?" and she lost the train of thought.

She met Jackson's eyes. "I was engaged to him."

Everyone was clearly stunned.

Jackson looked at Carter. "What?"

Carter nodded grimly. "This is Lacey Andrews. Garrett's fiancé."

Grimly. He most definitely looked grim. And for some reason that pissed her off. She thought they were maybe moving on. Okay, yes, they still had some things to work through regarding their feelings. But while things hadn't turned out the way any of them had expected, she *hated* that Carter wasn't talking about him and hadn't ever mentioned her name and was now *grim* about everyone knowing who she was.

"I need to go." She shoved her chair back and got to her feet. She stumbled past Nolan's big feet, her heart pounding. She went two steps then pivoted back to the table, stomped back, grabbed her coffee and then again turned and headed for the door.

Carter caught her before she even made it across the street.

"Lacey, stop."

She swung back to him. "I am Garrett's *ex*-fiance," she said, jamming her finger into his chest. "He died. So I can't really be his fiancé anymore, can I? I'm moving on and trying to be happy. Garrett is gone. And I'm okay talking about that and I'm also okay with *being* okay. I miss him. I get sad sometimes. But I'm not going to avoid talking about him and I'm not going to curl up into a little ball every time his name comes up. I'm not going to tiptoe around it and I'm not going to feel bad for wanting to be with you now. I don't care what your friends think. I *am* in love with you and—"

Carter kissed her.

Right in the middle of her rant, he grabbed her upper arms, pulled her to him and sealed his mouth over hers.

As soon as she sagged against him, he lifted a hand and ran it over her hair. He pulled back. "Shh, it's okay. Lace, it's all okay."

She gripped the front of his shirt. "I don't want to be sad anymore."

"I know. It's okay. I'm here."

"I want you, Carter"

"Okay."

"Okay?"

"Yes."

She pulled back a little. "Are you just saying that to calm me down so I don't make a scene?"

He looked around. They were in the middle of Main Street, on a busy Sunday morning. "Too late." He gave her a smile. "I'm saying it because it's true. It's all okay."

"We'll be together?"

"Yes. Anything you want."

"Really?" She felt her heart start thumping. She hadn't really thought that Carter would fight her. Not too hard anyway. But he was stubborn and sure of himself. She'd known it would be a battle.

"I love that you think I can make you happy," he said gruffly.

She frowned a little at those words. They weren't quite what she wanted. She wanted him to know that he *could* make her happy. Not just that she *thought so.*

"Carter, I…" But she trailed off. "You said I could stay for a while. So, date me, okay? Just you and me. Let's try it."

He pulled in a long breath but nodded. "I'll try."

"You will?"

"I want you to be happy, Lace. That's the main thing."

That was something. She still needed him to see that *he* would make her happy. That *he* was what she needed. But that would come with time.

She hoped.

"Okay. That's…good."

"Lacey?"

They both turned to find Annabelle coming toward them with a smile.

"I'm sorry about all of that," she said, waving toward the coffee shop. "We were just surprised."

Lacey let Carter go and stepped back. "And you're worried about Carter."

Annabelle smiled at him. "Sure, we are. He's our friend. But that doesn't mean we're worried about *you* being with Carter."

"Jackson is," Carter said. He gave a heavy sigh. "But he doesn't know the whole story."

Annabelle looked completely serious when she said, "Then go tell him. He cares about you, Carter. Fill him in."

Carter nodded. "Yeah, okay."

"And you and I," Annabelle said, looping her arm through Lacey's and turning her in the other direction. "Are going to go to my place and have mimosas and I'll tell you Carter and Garrett high school stories."

Lacey looked at Carter. He looked torn between worried and relieved.

It was a good sign he wanted his friends to like her, right?

And she did want to hear high school stories. "I love mimosas," she told Annabelle.

"And if I don't have stuff for those, we'll figure something out. Daiquiris have fruit in them and fruit is a late-Sunday-morning kind of thing, right?"

Oh, she and Annabelle could definitely be friends.

CHAPTER
SEVEN

"SO LACEY IS the reason you haven't had any serious relationships here?" Jackson asked as soon as Carter sat back down at the table.

He wasn't sure he wanted to have this conversation but he wasn't sure that he *didn't*. He wasn't sure that Jackson would let him get away with not having it anyway.

What he *was* sure of was that he needed more coffee.

"You knew there was a woman keeping him out of serious relationships here?" Nolan asked.

"No." Jackson looked a little put out at that. "He hasn't said a damned word about it. Her. Any of it. But I assume she's the reason?"

"It's…" Carter started. But how the hell did he explain all of this? "Complicated."

"Yeah, considering she was actually Big G's girl, I can see why that would be complicated," Jackson said dryly.

"She was…"

"What?" Nolan asked when Carter failed to go on.

Carter blew out a breath. "She was both of ours."

Nolan's eyebrows went up. "You were both sleeping with her? Did G know?"

"Of course he…no, we weren't…just the one…" Carter raked a hand through his hair. "It was…"

"Complicated?" Nolan supplied with a grin.

"Explain it," Jackson said simply. "Nolan and I are pretty sharp guys."

"Okay, fine. Fuck it. Garrett and I met her on the same night. The three of us hung out for over a year. A lot. I made a point of going to visit pretty often. I probably fell in love with her about the same time G did. But they lived in the same city and he was more fun and romantic, so he just naturally asked her to things often. He was better at the dating stuff than I ever would have been so it was a good set-up."

Jackson was watching him with more understanding in his eyes than Carter had ever seen. Jackson had been a wild ass in high school. But he'd left Bad for about ten years and had truly changed. He had spent the years since high school counseling at-risk teens. The idea that Jackson could see past whatever Carter was saying on the surface shouldn't surprise him, he supposed.

"So you had a perfect relationship," Jackson said. "You got to go down for the weekends, fuck and have fun, and then come home and let G deal with the real day-to-day stuff."

"Except that Garrett was the one who got to fuck her," Carter said, knowing he sounded stupid.

"So you were going to see them for…what?" Nolan asked.

"To hang out. Be with them."

"But you weren't *with* them?" Jackson asked.

"Nope. Though one night they offered a threesome. Turned out, I couldn't share her. Even though she wasn't mine to share." He shoved a hand through his hair.

Jackson seemed to be considering that.

"So what did you get out of it?" Nolan asked.

Carter shrugged. "Sounds stupid."

"Oh, say it anyway," Nolan said, with a grin.

"Fuck you, Winters," Carter muttered.

"Hey, seeing the big tough I-know-everything Carter Shaw

sounding stupid like the rest of us is kind of nice," Nolan said. "Come on. Tell us something stupid."

"Okay, fine. I wasn't getting laid down there, I knew my best friend was sleeping with the woman of my dreams, and I *still* didn't want to be anywhere but with her."

Nolan thought about that and then slowly shook his head. "Nope. Sorry, man. That doesn't sound stupid at all."

"No?" Carter asked crossly. "Because it *feels* stupid as shit."

"I agree with Nolan," Jackson said.

"You do?" Carter was definitely surprised.

"Yeah. I guess. I mean, I haven't felt that way about anyone but Annabelle...ever. But I guess I can see how it could happen."

Jackson sometimes surprised Carter with how articulate he'd become. And sometimes he didn't. But all of that was pretty damned enlightened for Jackson. Carter had to admit that ten years of growing up and then falling in love had done his friend some good.

"So you were in love with her and you went down, hung out, because you liked being with them. Because that was where you belonged. And now she's here, in love with you, wanting to be with you, and you're upset about that for some reason," Nolan summarized. "*That* is the stupid part."

"Yeah, well, you forgot about the part where Garrett is dead," Carter said bluntly.

"Yeah," Nolan said soberly. "I know, man. I'm sorry."

"You're feeling guilty," Jackson guessed. "For being with the woman Garrett loved now that he's dead."

"Kind of. Yes." Carter took a deep breath. "Two months before he died, I told him I thought he needed to break things off with her. I didn't think he was taking things seriously enough or that he was enough for her." He paused. "He proposed a week later. And was shot shortly after that." He shoved a hand through his hair. "Now that they're apart, like I wanted, I feel like hell."

"Like you're taking something that isn't yours?" Nolan asked.

"Maybe." But then Carter shook his head. "I feel like that's how I *should* feel. But I don't feel like she isn't mine."

Both of the other men raised their eyebrows.

That was the thing. It felt *right* with Lacey. In his gut. In his heart. It was his mind that was messing with him.

"Hell, I was considering moving back to Baton Rouge just before he died," Carter said.

"Oh," Jackson said simply.

"Really?" Nolan added.

Carter nodded. "I was still trying to wrap my head around it. If we could just keep going...kind of all dating and hanging out and maybe even sharing a bed. *How* it could work. But I just wanted to be there again." He swallowed hard. "But I took too long to get to yes."

Nolan frowned. "Okay. But Lacey's here now. She still wants to be with you."

"And I don't know if it will work without Garrett," Carter confessed.

Jackson sighed. "Because you don't think you can or want to do the marriage thing."

Everyone knew what a fuck up his dad was when it came to relationships. No one would be surprised to know that Carter shied away from commitment because of his father.

"I've seen marriage, up close and personal, turn into a miserable trap over and over," he said. "My dad makes women fall for him with big promises and gifts and romance and gets them bound to him legally as soon as possible. Then he smothers them. He wants to be with them constantly and doesn't want them to have other friends, he wants to provide everything for them, he wants to be their entire world. He's jealous and controlling. And when they get sick of it and claustrophobic and want out, he makes the legal battle and the divorce miserable."

"You'll never be like that," Jackson said. "There's no way."

"But I feel it with Lacey," Carter confessed.

"What?" Nolan asked.

"Like I want to possess her. Like I want to be her whole world. I was jealous of her and Garrett. Every damned time I saw them together."

"But you kept going down there and spending time with them," Nolan said.

"I couldn't stay away," Carter said, hating himself a little as he said it. "I wanted her so bad, but I needed Garrett to be the buffer. The guy kept me sane. He kept me from being the crazy jealous control freak."

"That doesn't make sense," Nolan said. "You know that."

"It does. I could only ever share a woman with someone I really liked and trusted. I didn't trust anyone more than the guy who had been my partner on the force and literally had my back every day. And Garrett was good for her, was everything I wasn't—fun and laid-back and easygoing. I'm too…intense and demanding. Just like my old man."

"Jesus, Carter," Jackson muttered. Then he leaned in and pinned Carter with a look. "You are *not* your father. Even if you hadn't seen that all up close and made a conscious choice to *not* be that guy, you wouldn't be. You're a good man and you don't need a buffer or whatever you think Garrett was."

Carter slapped his hand down on the table. "I feel it with her already," Carter insisted, feeling the sharp edge of anxiety that he was working to keep in check. "I want to be with her constantly, I want to wrap her up and keep her in my bed forever. I don't want her to go back to Baton Rouge…ever. I want to have her all to myself. It's like now that Garrett's gone and I don't *have* to share her, I don't want to even bring her to the coffee shop. Coming to town this morning was her idea."

"Oh, God. That's just love, man," Jackson said. "Wanting to be with her, wanting to keep her in your bed…that's all good stuff. That's how you should feel."

"I hesitated on moving back to Baton Rouge because I didn't

really want to share her and because I was afraid that over time it would wear on our friendship. I was afraid at some point I would make her choose, or that I would beat the shit out of Garrett or something. And now I lost the chance to actually give her a well-balanced relationship where she can have everything she wants and needs."

"You sound like a crazy person," Jackson said with a scowl.

"I fucking know that!" Carter looked around and lowered his voice. "I *feel* like a crazy person."

Jackson just shook his head.

It was Nolan who, calmly and rationally, said, "So let her stay for a while. Let her see what it's really like to be with you and all your craziness. And we'll keep you from proposing to her or actually tying her to your bed. Well, you know, for more than a few hours anyway."

Carter looked at Nolan. The guy was funny. He'd always known that, but Nolan had a confidence about him that he hadn't had in high school.

"She wants to stay. I already said yes. I can't *not* say yes to that woman."

"I know how that feels," Jackson said with a small smile. "That does not make you crazy."

"Or it makes *you* crazy too," Carter said.

Jackson thought about that, then nodded. "Point taken."

And that didn't make Carter feel one bit better.

On his way out to his truck, he decided he'd cook for Lacey that night. He wouldn't deny that impressing her was tempting and he was a good cook. He'd helped with grilling and stuff in Baton Rouge when he'd visited, but a lot of the time they'd gone out. If she was staying with him now, he'd have some great opportunities to show off his skills. In the kitchen. By cooking.

Good lord, was he ever going to be able to think of *anything* without it involving Lacey being naked?

He was just pulling his truck door open when he heard

someone call his name. He turned to see his dad's current girl-friend, Suzanne, coming toward him.

It wasn't as if he got close to his dad's women. Anymore. He'd learned not to get too attached. But he kind of liked Suzanne. She hadn't moved in with Matt—yet, anyway—hadn't given up her job to let Matt take care of her and she kind of gave Carter's old man a hard time. She was gorgeous, in an overdone, look-at-me kind of way, but she definitely had a body that, when dressed in her usual tight pants and skimpy tops, was worth looking at. She was also twenty-two years younger than his dad and could, honestly, have any single guy in town over the age of forty. What she was doing with Matt Shaw was beyond Carter. She'd claimed to actually love the guy when Carter had asked her. At that point, Carter had decided to stay out of it.

"Hey, Suzanne."

"He has my dog."

Carter hoped, for one second, that she wasn't talking about Matt. But she was. Who else would she be talking about?

"He has your dog where?"

"With him. I was out of town for a couple of days at a seminar and he agreed to take care of her. Now he won't give her back."

"And I assume you tried going over and just taking her?"

"I mean, he has her *with* him. Constantly. He takes her every-where. I went over yesterday to get her and he had her at the office with him. I waited until he got home but he wouldn't put her down at first, and then when he did, she followed him around everywhere. When I tried to pick her up, he blocked the door and wouldn't let me leave."

Carter ran a hand over his face. Jesus. His dad was such a child. But he was a physically big, fairly intelligent child. "What does he want?"

"Me to move in with him. Says Aphrodite wants to live with him."

Carter was distracted for a moment. "You named your dog Aphrodite?"

"He did. He gave her to me."

Uh-huh.

"He can't just keep her, right?"

"No, he can't. If he gave her to you as a gift, she's yours. Though I suppose he has ownership papers showing he actually paid for her?" Carter asked, knowing the answer. That was exactly the kind of dickhead, manipulative thing his dad would do. Get Suzanne emotionally attached to a dog that was actually, legally his and use it as leverage to get what he wanted from Suzanne.

"God, he's an ass," she groaned.

"He is. Why do you stay with him?"

She shrugged. "I love him. He's got a really good side too. He wants me to be happy, wants to take care of me. He just doesn't trust me not to leave."

Carter felt his gut clench at that. He wanted Lacey to be happy. He wanted to take care of her. He wanted her to never leave him.

For one brief millisecond of time, Carter thought back to how Lacey had liked that he'd taken Mooch in.

But then he shook his head. He would *not* use her affection for the cat to keep her around.

"Your mom did a number on him," Suzanne said. "It's not really his fault."

Carter scowled at her. "Stop making excuses for him. If you want your dog back, I'll go with you, but you have to be tough on him."

She drew herself up straight and nodded. "Yes, okay, I'm in. I want my dog back."

Carter opened his door and gestured for her to climb in. She did, sliding over the seat to the passenger side. Carter went in after her.

They drove over to his dad's house, Carter's childhood

home, in silence. He'd made this drive before, just with a different woman in the front seat. Twice before, actually. Both times in his capacity as a police officer rather than Matt's son, but he hadn't wanted any of the other cops to get involved. This was embarrassing enough.

The first time, he'd taken Lilly over to get the rest of her things—a television, some dishes and a coffee table—that she hadn't taken when she'd first moved out. Matt had let her in the house each time she'd gone over but had cried and begged and pleaded when she tried to leave, and the last time had actually shut her in the bedroom for almost an hour without her cell phone. She'd finally broken a window and climbed out.

The second time had been with Donna, and she'd come to Carter as soon as she decided to move out. He'd gone with her and kept his dad away from her while she'd loaded up her stuff. Thankfully, her stuff had all been things she could carry out herself in a matter of about thirty minutes.

This time… God only knew what it would be like. A dog. A living thing. That apparently was attached to Matt and that Matt maybe legally owned.

Carter was so glad Lacey was with Annabelle and wouldn't see this.

As he pulled up in the driveway, blocking in his dad's car, Carter grabbed his cell and tapped out a quick text to both Lacey and Annabelle, saying he'd had a work call and could Annabelle take Lacey back to his place when they were done.

Then he got out of the truck and prepared to face his father.

The big man who had never laid a finger on Carter and had, by most counts, been a decent father, if not a great role model for male-female relationships, met them on the porch. He was holding a tiny fluffy white dog in his arms.

"You didn't have to bring Carter," he said to Suzanne.

She glared at him. "You were going to just hand her over if I came over by myself?"

"I told you that you are free to visit her anytime you want, babe."

"I don't want to visit her, you jackass. I want to *have* her."

"Move in and she's all yours."

"Dad," Carter interrupted. "Do you have papers showing ownership?"

"Of course I do." He stroked the dog's head.

"I'm going to need to see them."

Matt turned and headed back inside. "Well, come on then."

Carter looked at Suzanne. "You want to stay out here?"

"No." She started for the porch.

"You have to realize, if he's got papers with only his name on them, there's not much I can do but try to talk to him."

"I understand," she said.

Carter followed her into the house, through the living room and into the kitchen, where Matt had the dog on the counter drinking from a little dish of water. Carter rolled his eyes. Matt wasn't exactly the tiny-fluffy-dog type.

"Here you go." Matt handed Carter an envelope. Inside were, indeed, ownership papers indicating that Aphrodite was Matt's dog.

Carter sighed. His dad was in the right, legally. But he was still being a dick.

He passed the papers to Suzanne. "I'm sorry."

She didn't even glance at them.

"Give me my dog," she said to Matt.

"She's happy. Well cared for. Why can't you let me do the same for you?" he asked.

Suzanne snorted. "You're comparing me to a dog, Matt."

"A dog I love."

Suzanne gave him a warning look. "You might want to think about your words before you say them out loud."

"I need her here," Matt said. "If you're not here with me, I need this reminder of you."

Carter sighed—and firmly squelched *any* thought of *I know how you feel.*

God, he was pathetic. Lacey had been in his house less than twenty-four hours. True, he'd always recognized that seeing her in Baton Rouge was better because having memories of her here, in his town, his house and his *bed*, would torture him after she left. But as much as he knew he'd miss her, if she wanted to leave, he'd let her. Of course. He might nicely ask her to stay. He might give her a key and tell her she was welcome absolutely anytime. But that was it. He was not going to beg her to stay. He would not try to manipulate her into wanting to be with him.

Probably.

But damn if in that moment with his dad, Carter didn't wonder if being a devious bastard was genetic.

"Matt, if you lighten up and relaxed a little, I'll want to be here *more*. And I'll bring her over with me every time," Suzanne said.

"But you're not here *all the time*," Matt said. He picked the dog up again, holding her against his chest. "I want to wake up with you and go to sleep with you every single day for the rest of my life."

That sounded damn familiar as well.

"Dad," Carter broke in crossly. "This isn't how you treat people you care about. Suzanne is a grown woman with her own life. She knows what she wants. She's amazing—sweet, intelligent, funny, beautiful. You should be damn glad she wants to spend even five minutes with you. Quit being an asshole, give her the dog, and be the guy she *wants* to be with, rather than a guy she just can't get away from."

Matt and Suzanne both stared at him with wide eyes.

Carter was a little surprised himself.

And okay, maybe he'd been talking about him and Lacey in there too. Still, it was all true and he stood by it.

"She makes me crazy," Matt finally muttered.

"I know," Carter said. And he did. It was probably the first moment of his adult life where he actually felt a connection with his father as a man and not just his dad. "But wouldn't you rather have her here because she *wants* to be here, instead of because you've made it impossible for her to leave?"

He felt that realization hit hard too. Lacey *was* here because she wanted to be. He'd never controlled or manipulated her. He'd been damned careful not to. So he'd have to work on it from here, but she was in Bad, right now, for him. In spite of him trying to keep his distance and *not* put any pressure on her. She was insistent on staying when all he'd done was think about how she shouldn't.

A surge of relief went through him. And shock that his father, of all people, had helped him see all of this.

"Yeah, okay." Matt handed Aphrodite over to Suzanne. "But I'd love it if you would come over more often and maybe stay the night once in a while."

Suzanne moved in, the dog cradled in one arm, the other around Matt. She kissed his cheek. "All you have to do is ask nicely."

Matt nodded. "Okay."

Carter sighed. Suzanne would be better off just walking away, but Carter could only do so much. "So, the dog is Suzanne's?" he asked.

"Yes," Matt said.

"Suzanne, you might want to get some paperwork drawn up to that effect."

Matt frowned. "That's not necessary."

Uh-huh.

"I'm not worried," Suzanne said, smiling up at her boyfriend.

Carter fought the urge to groan. She shouldn't trust Matt.

"I'm not going anywhere," she said to Matt. "And you'll learn that and trust it eventually. But not if I let you bully me into it."

Matt actually looked contrite. "I just love you so damned much."

"I know." She kissed his cheek again. "It's my love for you that's in question. But stick around—you'll figure it out."

Carter was amazed. Not only by Suzanne's words but by the look on his dad's face. Matt really wanted to believe her, Carter could see it. And suddenly he hoped that Suzanne had the staying power to prove to Matt that he could be loved.

Carter cleared his throat. "I'll give you and Aphrodite a ride home," he told Suzanne.

"No, I'm okay. We're going to stay here."

He'd been expecting that answer. "Okay. Let me know if you need anything else."

"Hey, Carter," his dad called as he started for the door.

He looked back. "Yeah?"

"Heard your girlfriend's in town. Good for you."

"Uh, thanks. Maybe we'll stop by so you can meet her sometime."

"I'd like that."

Carter got to the front door before his dad called again, "Hey, son?"

"Yeah?"

"You don't want her to get away. Get a ring on her finger."

Carter felt his optimism dry up like a spilled drink in the desert. Because he lived his life doing the opposite of *What Would Matt Shaw Do?*

CHAPTER
EIGHT

"YOU HAD FUN WITH ANNABELLE?" Carter asked.

Lacey was sitting on a stool across from where Carter was cooking. The stovetop was set into the island in the middle of the kitchen with a huge expanse of marble on all sides, making it the perfect cooking space.

He was making fajitas.

And she loved him even more for it.

She reached out and snagged a piece of red pepper from the plate where he had all the ingredients ready for cooking. "Yeah, she's great."

"How many daiquiris did you have?" he asked.

Lacey grinned. "Only two."

He laughed. "You took a long nap when you got back."

"Well, that might not have been just because of the daiquiris. I was up late last night."

He gave her a wink and her heart tripped.

This was a different man than she'd expected to come home to. Things had been intense that morning and she'd known he hadn't wanted to take her to Bad Habit. He'd been guarded the whole time they'd been there, even though they'd been with his friends.

But she didn't regret what she'd said to him. She wasn't going to miss out on a great love because the man was stubborn and feeling guilty.

She knew that he would have been okay with her spending only the weekend in Bad and not leaving the house, or getting dressed, until she got in her car to go back to Baton Rouge. But she wanted, *needed,* more and she really believed that being the one to give her what she needed was what Carter needed too.

If she had left, she'd like to think he would have resumed his trips to Baton Rouge on weekends to see her. She'd like to think that now that they'd seen each other again, he wouldn't be able to resist phone calls and funny text messages like they used to have. She'd like to think the desire to see her as often as possible would have been too much to resist.

But she'd realized sometime between leaving her apartment in Baton Rouge and driving down Main Street, Bad next to Carter that she wasn't going back to Baton Rouge. Her family was there. But she could visit. What she really wanted and needed was here.

"What did you talk about for all that time?" Carter asked as he transferred the veggies into the pan to sauté them.

The question seemed casual but she knew it wasn't. He wanted to know what she'd told Annabelle about them.

She and Annabelle had talked for almost two hours. They'd had a really nice time. They hadn't talked about anything heavy. There had been no talk of Garrett's death or their relationship. True to her word, Annabelle had told stories of high school, and even some before high school. She'd grown up in Bad and had known Garrett and Carter her whole life. She'd even pulled out old yearbooks.

"I heard about the time you were caught making out with the head cheerleader in Coach's office," she said.

Carter chuckled. "Randi," he said. "She dared me."

"And she's the local mechanic?" Lacey asked.

"Yep. She can fix anything with a motor."

Lacey had to admit she was impressed by that. She knew nothing about cars. "So she was kind of a tomboy?" she asked. That didn't seem like Carter's type. At least not if Lacey was Carter's type. She was definitely *not* a tomboy.

Carter laughed and slid the vegetables onto a platter, adding the steak to the pan next. "Uh, I guess kind of. She knows more about football than a lot of the guys on the team. She's a mechanic. She swears like a sailor and can probably drink a lot of my friends under the table. But she was still girlie somehow. Head cheerleader. Favorite color is purple. Always looks amazing."

Lacey frowned, feeling a twinge of jealousy that was stupid. "You like her."

He looked up. He read something in her expression and smiled. "I do like her. I've known her since preschool. She's a great girl. And," he added, bracing his hands on the counter and pinning her with an intent look, "if I wanted to be with her, I would be. We messed around in high school a few times. Just like every other girl here, no one interested me long term."

She liked that. And knew her jealousy was stupid. Of course Carter had been with women before her. Hell, even during the year she'd known him and had been with Garrett. But she'd never thought about him being serious with anyone. Because she'd been unable to imagine *her* life without him.

"Because you never thought you wanted to be long-term with anyone at all," she said.

He nodded. "Except you."

Her heart thumped hard against her ribs. *That* was what she wanted to hear. "You do want to be with me long-term?"

"More than anything I've ever wanted in my life, Lace."

She felt tears sting her eyes. "Carter, I—"

"And that's what scares me about it."

"Scares you? Why?"

"There's just…stuff you don't know."

She pressed her lips together and absorbed that. She

shouldn't be surprised, probably, but she was. "I thought I knew you really well."

"You do. But there are things I didn't want you to know. Things you didn't need to know."

"And I didn't need to know why you felt the way you did about long-term relationships because you didn't think we'd ever have one."

He didn't divert his gaze or sugarcoat it. He just nodded.

"Will you tell me now?" she asked.

"Yes. Because I want you to know it's not because I don't want it." He took a deep breath. "I might want it too much."

Lacey smiled in spite of the fact that he was essentially still holding back. "We're both going to make mistakes, Carter. But if we want this, that's what matters."

He took a long, deep breath and nodded. "I can try. Later. Let's eat first."

Her stomach rumbled on cue. "You have a soft spot for a stray cat and you can cook," she said. "What more can I ask for?"

He looked like he was going to respond to that, but instead he smiled. "Stray cats and fajitas. Easy."

They had a wonderful dinner—Carter really was a great cook—and as they moved out onto his back patio with glasses of iced tea, Lacey realized how much this was like their weekends in Baton Rouge.

And it didn't make her sad, just a little sentimental.

Their conversation was easy and nonspecific at first. She curled up on the reclining patio chair and Carter took the chair next to her. They both watched the fireflies as they talked and laughed and fell into comfortable silences.

The air was cool enough that the fire felt great, but she didn't need a jacket and Lacey felt herself relaxing into the chair and growing drowsy. It had been only twenty-four hours since she'd shown up in Bad but it felt as if she'd been here for a month or more. It just all felt right.

Carter lifted a remote control, and hit a button. Music floated over the patio from hidden speakers.

"Nice," she said. She paused to listen. Then laughed. "Just happens to be Chase Rice?" she asked.

He chuckled too. "Pure coincidence."

She rolled her head to look at him. "You don't need Chase Rice music to make me horny, Carter."

"I know that."

"I forgot who I was talking to—Mr. Confident himself."

"But I heard that three Chase Rice songs in and you're bare naked and ready to go."

Her eyebrows shot up. "You heard that, huh?"

He grinned unapologetically. "Not that I'm surprised. I know that you've had four orgasms a week, minimum, ever since you turned twenty-one."

"You remember me saying that?" She'd confessed that a long time ago. "That was when my friends took me to that sex store for my birthday and got me my first vibrator."

Carter groaned. "Do you know how hard that night was?"

She giggled. "No pun intended?"

"Totally intended," he said. "That was the first night I jerked off thinking about you."

She sat up straighter in the chair. "Really?"

"I'd resisted up 'til then, just thinking it was wrong to do that when you were Garrett's girl, but damn, I never would have gotten any sleep."

"I love that story," she breathed.

He looked over at her. "It was the first of many times after that. Kind of like the dam broke."

She knew what he meant. She'd had some fantasies going herself.

"We had some of the craziest conversations," she said. "I was always amazed at the things you and Garrett could get me to talk about. I wondered for a while if he put weed on the fire or something."

Carter grinned. "Does weed make you talkative?"

She shrugged. "I don't know. Never tried it. I'm pretty talkative anyway."

He nodded. "Garrett always steered those conversations if you think about it. You and I participated, but he always started them."

Thinking about it now, she realized he was right. "He was always trying to make it sexual with us. I thought it was because he liked getting me worked up like that before bedtime."

"I'm sure that was some of it," Carter said dryly. "God, the first night I stayed over and didn't bring my earphones was hell."

She gasped and reached out to swat his arm. "Stop it. We weren't loud."

"No, you two weren't loud. *You* were loud."

She blushed but laughed. "Nuh-uh."

"Lacey, you're loud in bed. And it's the best stuff I've ever heard."

Just like that the moment got intense and heated.

"You brought your headphones after that?" she asked.

"I didn't always use them."

"So you listened? And jerked off?"

He gave her a sexy half smile and her stomach flipped as her whole body got hot.

"And I'll have you know, I outlasted both of you," he said.

She laughed. "Duly noted."

He looked out over the yard. "God, you were insatiable. Every night, every time I was in town."

She bit her lip for a moment, not sure if she should tell him what she was about to say. In the end, she blurted, "*Because* you were in town."

He looked over again. "What?"

"I mean, we had sex when you weren't in town of course," she said. "But I stayed over at his place and we had sex every night you were there *because* you were there."

He narrowed his eyes. "Why?"

"Maybe because we were always drinking and laughing and having such fun. Or because the conversations always got naughty eventually. Or because I had this fantasy that you *would* hear us and come in and join us."

She could feel the heat coming from him even over the two or three feet that separated their chairs.

"You have no idea how many times I thought about that."

"But you never did."

"I didn't know…" He stopped. "That's not true. I knew what would happen. It was the morning after that I wasn't sure about."

She got that.

"So what did you do while I was at Annabelle's?" she asked, watching the pinks and oranges in the sky fading.

He didn't respond for a beat, then said, "Took care of something for…work…for a bit, went to the store for dinner stuff and came home."

"I suppose you're on twenty-four-seven as a cop in a small town."

"Yeah, seems that way sometimes. But this was…"

He trailed off and she looked over at him. "It was what?"

"It had to do with my dad."

Suddenly her drowsiness disappeared. There was something in his tone that alerted her this was important. "Okay."

He was still studying the yard and Lacey turned in her chair to do the same rather than looking at him, hoping that might make it easier for him to open up.

"My mom left when I was two. My dad was madly in love with her, crazy, over-the-top in love. He adored her, worshipped her, lived for her. She was a free spirit and didn't believe in marriage. Believed that marriage was nothing more than a piece of paper and had nothing to do with a real committed relationship. So they never did it officially."

He paused to take a drink of his iced tea and Lacey made herself keep all of her questions inside.

It was tough.

"They were together for a couple of years before I was born and everything was great, I guess. That's what everyone says anyway. My dad won't even say her name."

Lacey was proud of the way she casually sipped her tea and kept her seat even when she felt as if something was pulling her to go put her arms around him.

"Anyway, after that, my dad was pretty messed up about relationships with women. He was always good to me. We had a great time together. But I had three stepmothers before I was fifteen."

"Whoa." Lacey couldn't help blurting the word out but quickly pressed her lips together and motioned for him to go on.

He gave her a little smile that made her breathe easier though.

"I didn't really understand all the issues until my third stepmom left and I started paying attention. Dad is…always has been…really…*desperate*, I guess, about women. He goes over-board on everything. First date, Valentine's Day, birthdays, anniversaries, proposals. Crazy, romantic, expensive stuff. He'll do anything for the woman he's currently in love with."

Lacey was fascinated. She couldn't help it. "But he falls out of love easily too?" she asked.

Carter laughed at that. "Oh Jesus, no. He's all in one hundred and ten percent forever."

"So why all the women?"

"He drives them crazy." Carter sighed. "He's romantic and sweet until he gets them down the aisle. Then he's clingy and jealous and controlling. They're bound to him then, or so he thinks, and he believes he's in love with them but he's so damned scared of them leaving that he becomes obsessed with making them happy."

"That sounds…" Lacey wasn't sure.

"Right?" Carter said. "Like how can it be bad that he wants them to be happy? But he wants to be the center of their universe like he's made them the center of his."

"And eventually they can't take it anymore," Lacey guessed.

"And then he does absolutely everything in his power to keep them from leaving him. It gets seriously crazy. And I clean a lot of it up. As a cop, I'm able to, and I like to keep as much private as I can. Though in Bad, you can imagine a lot of it gets out."

"Clean it up how?" Lacey asked.

"Believe it or not, I've helped two women get restraining orders against my dad. I've arrested him for violating one of them. I've physically restrained him while a woman moved out on him. That kind of stuff."

"Wow." Lacey sank back in her chair. "I'm sorry you have to do all that."

"It's one of the reasons I moved back to Bad," he said. "I thought maybe I could keep his craziness under control."

They sat for a few quiet seconds, each thinking.

"The other reason was you."

She whipped her head to look at him. "I'm the other reason you moved back here?"

"Yep."

"But…why? It was so fun. We saw you so much more often. You and Garrett were so close."

"Exactly. It was too much. Seeing you together, feeling the way I did, I knew I needed to get some distance."

Lacey wrapped her arms around herself and thought about that. It kind of hurt, frankly.

After a moment Carter went on. "I never wanted to be serious long term with someone because to me, marriage was what always made everyone unhappy. Dad kind of behaved while he was just dating someone. I mean, a few women got tired of his jealousy and stuff early on and never made it to the diamond ring, but the ones he did marry—it seemed like they were happy up until then. They had their own lives and friends and jobs and stuff. Dad was part of their lives, but wasn't their *whole* life. Like a normal relationship. But as soon as they had his ring and last name, suddenly they stopped seeing their friends and their family, he made three of them quit their jobs, saying he wanted to support them and that they were taking away his chance to provide for them and care for them. He wanted to know where they were all the time and who they were with. It was just...so toxic. And for several years, I thought that was marriage. I didn't see any other marriages behind closed doors. I just saw my dad claiming to love my stepmoms and them being miserable. And I never wanted any of that."

Lacey shuddered slightly. Obviously Carter's dad had some issues. Those marriages were in no way typical. But thinking that all of that had been Carter's reality for a long time made her sad—for the little boy who hadn't seen true love up close and for the man who clearly still had some scars from it.

She pushed up out of her chair and slid into his lap before she could think twice about it. Carter might not want her comfort but he was going to get it. She sat sideways on his thighs and put her hands on his shoulders. "You're not your dad."

He set his glass to one side and put his hands on her hips. "I know. I've always felt very much not like my dad. I've never understood him."

There was a long, heavy pause and Lacey held her breath.

"Until you."

Lacey felt her heart drop. She frowned. "What do you mean?"

"I've never loved someone so much that I wanted to be the only thing that made her smile, the first thing she thinks of in the morning, the person she wants to share everything with. But I get it now."

"With me?" Lacey asked softly.

"I want to consume you. I want to make you mine in every

way and I don't want you to ever need or want anything I can't give you."

Lacey felt her lips part and her breathing speed up. She knew that he was saying all of this as a warning, a way to scare her off, but it wasn't working.

"And you love me?"

"I'm crazy about you," he said. Then he chuckled. "And that's what I'm worried about."

She put her hands to his face, making him look at her. "Being in love isn't crazy."

"Lacey…I can't even explain it." He sighed, clearly frustrated. Then said, "Watching you eat my cooking tonight made me hard."

She felt her eyes widen. "Really?"

"Making something for you that you enjoyed that much…it was almost like sex." His hands squeezed her hips. "I fucking loved providing that for you, doing that for you. If it hadn't been insane, I probably would have insisted on actually feeding you."

She felt a smile threatening but he was definitely worked up about this and she had to take it seriously. "I spent the morning with Annabelle and you were fine with that."

He nodded. "Yeah."

"And you would never try to cut me off from my family."

"No."

"Or make me quit my job."

He hesitated over that one.

"Carter?"

"No. I wouldn't. It's just that if you moved here, you wouldn't have a job and that would be okay with me."

"I'd figure something out. I love what I do and I'm not the type to sit around and just wait for my man to get home."

His fingers tightened on her hips at her words.

"Oh, you like the 'my man' thing?" she asked, wiggling a little closer to his fly.

"I do. I want to be your everything. And Jesus, Lace, I actually *get* my dad. I see how this could become an obsession. The idea of you leaving makes me want to howl."

"But most of all, you want me to be happy," she said.

"Yes."

"And I would be *unhappy* if I didn't have my friends, family and job and a few interests and hobbies outside of you. So you won't do that to me."

He looked up at her and she could see that his emotions were still swirling. But he wanted to agree with her.

"I can't marry you," he finally said roughly. "I don't want kids. I've seen divorce rip people up and I know people stay because of the kids all the time. I don't want you bound to me in any way. I want you here because you want to be here. I want you here because of how you feel. I don't want there to be any other reasons. And I want you to be free to leave whenever you want to."

Lacey felt her stomach knot.

He saw it in her face.

"And *this* is why I loved having Garrett as a part of this. He was that guy. The husband-and-father guy. I want you to have that but I can't be the one to give it. But now, without him, I don't want you to be with anyone else. But I know that you want it and I want to give you everything..." He blew out a frustrated breath. "I'm so fucked up over this."

Lacey swallowed hard and put her finger over his lips. "It's okay."

He started to shake his head but she pressed against his lips. "Yes, Carter. It's okay. I showed up here just last night. We have time to figure it all out. Part of all of this is still the emotions over Garrett and being apart for so long and now that we're together, everything is jumbled up. We'll work it out." She moved her finger and leaned in, putting her lips to his is a gentle kiss. "What I do know is that there's nowhere else for me to be. I *need* to be here with you." She kissed him again, a little longer and harder this time, then said, "And if

I'm going to be consumed by someone, I definitely want it to be you."

He groaned and lifted a hand to the back of her head, taking over the kiss this time, urging her lips open and stroking his tongue boldly over hers. Then he growled, "Woman, those are dangerous words."

"I mean every one of them."

He kissed her again, hungrily, and she pressed her butt against his cock.

When he let her go he said, "Do you know how many times we've sat by a fire pit and all I could do was think about how gorgeous you would look with me thrusting into you by firelight?"

She whimpered as need seemed to seep into her bones. "As many times as I've watched you sitting on the other side of the fire pit and imagined getting up, walking over to you, stripping as I went, then climbing onto your lap and riding you?" she asked.

He went still for a moment. Then he gripped her hips and pushed her off of his lap. "Do that."

She got to her feet. "Really?"

"Yes. Holy shit, yes."

A thrill went through her. She really had imagined this scenario countless times. Whether he'd been pissed off over the way the Cowboys had played or laughing while telling some dumb criminal story, she remembered watching him across the patio and imagining exactly what she'd just described.

Lacey walked to the opposite edge of the patio. She turned back and met his eyes. She held the eye contact as she started toward him slowly. She tugged her top off and tossed it onto the closest chair. She toed one shoe off, then the other and kicked them out of the way. Her shorts were next, tossed to drape over the arm of the chair she'd been sitting in. Then her bra. By the time she was directly in front of him she wore only her tiny bikini panties, and she pushed those down and stepped out of them as she put a knee on each side of his on the chair cushion.

Still watching his face, she pushed his shirt up to bare the abs she'd always fantasized about and stroked her hand over the hard ridges.

His breath hissed out at the first contact and his fingers dug into the arms of the chair.

The firelight shone in his dark eyes and she could see the tightness in his jaw as he held himself in check. She unbuttoned and unzipped him, pulling his shorts and underwear out of the way and wrapping a hand around his cock.

"I imagined you exactly like this. That you would be hard and hot just sitting here talking and laughing with me."

"Every damned time, babe."

She loved that—the words, the truth she could hear, the roughness in his voice that spoke to how much she was effecting him.

"Did you know that every time you laugh it goes right through me, like brandy on a cold night? It just rushes through me and makes me feel hot and happy but also needy, like I'd do absolutely anything you asked."

"Fuck, Lace," he ground out, pushing his cock up into her grip.

"Oh, yeah, move against me like that," she urged, tightening around him.

He groaned and flexed his hips again. The feel of him sliding through her fingers made her wet and she was throbbing with the need for him after only three strokes. But she didn't want to let go of him.

"You better move your hand and get on," he told her. "You're too good at that."

"I'd love to see you come like this," she said, not taking her eyes off of her hand around him.

"God, woman, you're going to kill me." He grabbed her hips and pulled her forward. "Sometime. No problem. But not this time. The first time I come with you on a patio like in all of my dirty daydreams, it's gonna be buried deep inside your sweet pussy and with you coming hard on my cock while I fill you up."

She almost orgasmed right then and there. But he lifted her and then brought her down on him, easing into her as if they had been made to fit together.

She grabbed his shoulders, his name coming out in a long moan as she took every inch of him.

He gave her no time to even breathe again before he was lifting her and thrusting again. She took the cue and began moving up and down, taking him deep and then rising almost to the tip before going down again.

It was magnificent.

The fresh air, the firelight, the stars overhead and Carter's hard, hot body, her name on his lips as he struggled to breathe.

They came together.

It shouldn't be that easy. Lacey knew that. But as she sagged against Carter and felt his hand stroking up and down her back, heard his heart beating under her ear, as intimately connected as two people could be, she didn't care if it was easy or not—it was worth it.

THREE WEEKS.

Lacey had been in Bad for three weeks and Carter was already so used to her being there—at his dinner table, in his bed, on his couch, under his cat, that he knew without a doubt, with absolute certainty, only one thing: he was royally fucked.

They'd been laughing, loving, talking, and getting closer every day for three weeks and he never wanted to let her go.

He hadn't wanted to let her go from the moment he'd met her. But he had. Kind of. Now he couldn't. The best he could do now was not become a crazy, controlling freak.

Easier said than done.

He'd been doing okay until she'd gotten sick. But for the past week or so she'd been not feeling well and had spent the last two days lying in bed or kneeling beside the toilet.

It was making him nuts to not be able to make things better, but the last two days had been his days off and at least he'd been there with her. Today he was working and it was making him, well, crazy.

Carter shook his head and tried to force himself to focus on the report in front of him. There wasn't anything he could do for her and, honestly, she didn't *need* him to do anything. It was a stomach bug. She had soup and crackers and Netflix and Mooch. She just needed to get through it. And *he* needed to get some damned perspective.

But this was exactly why he was so sure he was completely fucked.

Things had been great. Comfortable. Familiar. Hot. Sweet. For two weeks. He'd had her all to himself, his feelings of guilt had faded and he'd started to believe that things could be normal between them.

When he was at work, she hung out at home with Mooch, cooking, reading, doing some work remotely and relaxing. She'd even gone down to Bad Brews with some of his friends a couple of times. She fit in, she liked it here, everyone liked *her*.

It was all good.

He was keeping his shit together. He was settling in. He was confident about how she felt about him and that he could maybe even possibly be the guy she needed him to be.

And then she got sick.

Of course, he'd realized on some level that he was completely overreacting to some basic puking. This was nothing in the overall scheme. But he'd had this helpless, I-need-to-be-with-her-constantly feeling nagging at him ever since he'd awakened at three a.m. the first morning to hear her retching in the bathroom.

He clearly couldn't be rational about the woman he loved any more than his father had ever been. And the last thing Carter wanted was to make Lacey miserable the way his father made the women in his life.

Carter tamped that thought and tried to unknot his gut. It was all ridiculous. He couldn't explain why he was so worked up over her throwing up a little. She didn't have a fever. She actually felt pretty good most of the day. It was just when the nausea hit and she couldn't stop puking that he felt as if he was going to crawl out of his skin.

He should be happy to be at work, distracted by something

other than the instinctual need to take care of Lacey every goddamned minute of the day.

"Shaw!"

Carter looked toward his chief's office doorway. "Yeah?"

"In here."

Carter shoved his chair back and stood quickly.

Thank God.

He couldn't distract himself but maybe something big had happened. He shouldn't be hoping for a call that would take all of his attention and time for the rest of his shift but…he was. He really was.

"Tonight could get rowdy. Steve already called and said that some kids were mouthing off to each other at the gas station," Don Keaton, the Chief of Police, said as Carter stepped into his office.

Tonight was the big season opener against Autre, the Bad Renegades' biggest rivals. That meant there would be a lot of football players jacked up on testosterone, ex-football players jacked up on testosterone and football players' dads jacked up on testosterone.

Grown men often got stupid when it came to sports and there was no sport like football in Bad, Louisiana, and the surrounding area. High school rivalries lasted forever around here. It wasn't unheard of for a guy to not get a job somewhere because of where he'd played ball and a romance between kids from rival towns was like a damned Romeo and Juliet story. It was ridiculous. And it made Carter grin as he strode into his boss's office. He felt the same way. No kid of his would ever date someone from Autre.

His grin dropped. Well, he didn't have to worry about that.

No kid of his would ever date someone from Autre…because there wouldn't be any kids of his.

He'd always told himself that. Or at least ever since figuring out that his mother had stayed with his dad two years longer than she would have otherwise because of *him*.

Lacey would *never* leave a kid. In fact, he was beginning to think that she would stay with him forever because of a stray cat.

But he couldn't tie her down like that. He *wouldn't*. If Lacey stayed with him, it would be because she wanted to, never because she felt as though that was her only option.

He shoved those thought aside and focused on his boss.

"Yeah. Afterward could be interesting too," Carter agreed. Last year the rivalry game had been in Autre and there had been a couple of fights, a stolen car and a spray-painted building in the aftermath of Autre's big win.

This year was even bigger. Bad was on track to do something they hadn't done since Carter, Garrett, Jackson, Luke, Marc, and Jase had played—bring home the state championship trophy.

And no one wanted to bring them down more than Autre.

"I know you need to be at the game for the halftime ceremony," Don said.

Carter and the rest of the championship team had been invited to go onto the field with Coach Karr for a special presentation to the coach who had meant so much to so many. Carter and the rest of the guys were really looking forward to it.

"Yeah. Why?"

"Was hoping you'd be willing to be at the game in uniform," Don said. "I know you're there as a guest tonight, but it would be helpful to have the badge visible in case of any trouble."

Carter knew Don was right. And he didn't mind. It wasn't like everyone didn't know who he was anyway, including those from Autre, but somehow the uniform often helped keep people in check.

"That's fine."

"You mind patrolling a little while you're there rather than sitting in the stands?" Don asked. "Greg and Lance will be there too. And Landry will be there on the other side and will help keep things in line."

Carter had been planning to sit with Lacey among their friends—*their* friends, he liked the sound of that—but he realized that Lacey likely wouldn't be attending the game now with the way she was feeling. Which shouldn't disappoint him. He wasn't playing and it wasn't *him* that was getting the award tonight. But he was damn proud of being a part of the championship team and the idea of taking the field with his teammates and coach again had been great. The idea of having Lacey see him strutting his stuff with the other guys who could still rehash every detail of every play of that final big game had made him grin.

Now he might as well patrol during the game. "Sure. Not a problem."

"Great. Appreciate it."

"Absolutely."

Carter finished up the report he'd been working on and then headed out. He knew the places where the Bad kids were most likely to run into kids from Autre and start trouble.

As he cruised the streets, he called Lacey.

"Hi."

Her voice made him smile, as always. "You sound better."

"I am," she agreed. "I don't feel like eating, but I have a lot more energy."

"I'm glad."

"I'm even feeling up for the game tonight."

"Nah." He turned into the ice cream shop on the edge of town. School would be letting out in about ten minutes and this would be the first stop for a lot of the kids. "I agreed to patrol tonight so you can just stay home and rest."

"What about the halftime stuff?" she asked. "You have to be there."

She knew how much this meant to him. He'd shared stories with her, not only of the glory days of playing and their amazing senior season, but about how important Coach was to a lot of the kids in town, particularly Carter's teammates. It warmed him that she understood this was a big deal. In the overall scheme of things, did one high school football coach in one small town in

Louisiana really matter? He did in Carter's opinion. Coach Karr had influenced so many guys who had gone on to influence other people and so on. The ripple effect was obvious to Carter and the other guys, but they were looking forward to showing it to everyone by surrounding Coach on that football field tonight and thanking him for everything he'd done. Not only would the community see it, but Nolan was writing a piece on the whole thing for the paper in San Antonio that he was confident would get picked up by the Associated Press.

"I'll be patrolling *at* the game," he told her. "Keeping an eye on the crowd."

"Oh, good. Then I'll still see you."

He shook his head even though she couldn't see it. "Lace, you should stay home and rest."

"I feel so much better though," she protested. "I'd really love to be there."

And he wanted her there. He really did. In fact…it would feel strange if she wasn't there. Which made no sense. Lacey had never been with him at a Bad football game before. How could it feel weird to *not* have her there? But he knew.

He was in love with her.

Which meant he was at risk for making a huge mess out of everything.

"Can you go with someone?" he asked. "In case you start not feeling good?"

"Of course," she said.

"Okay," he conceded. "I'd love to have you there."

She gave a little squeal that made him smile.

"But I won't be able to sit with you," he said with some regret. He wanted to sit on his stadium blanket and hold her hand and cheer the team on with her and the rest of his friends. But the patrol was important too.

"Maybe we can meet up behind the bleachers and make out for a little while," she teased. "But don't worry about the game. I'll be fine with everyone else."

Everyone else. His friends. The men and women who were practically like siblings. They were the people he trusted and counted on and wanted to be with each day. The people who had his back and who made him a better man. She was a part of them. Already. Or finally. Or…something.

And the more he thought about Lacey being friends with Annabelle and Regan and Randi, the better he felt. Those girls knew and cared about and stuck by some of the most hard-headed men he knew. Maybe they could help Lacey stick through it when *he* fucked up. Because he was going to. For sure.

And hell, Jackson and Nolan already knew that Carter was on the borderline of crazy obsessive about Lacey. They could keep him sane. Yes, this would be good. These guys had always been his team on and off the field.

"And if you're feeling up to it, we'll hit the after-party Elyse is putting together out at Jase's new place," he said.

"Oh, yes! That would be great."

She sounded sincerely excited and Carter smiled again. It would be great. He'd make sure it was.

"Okay, gotta go. See you soon," he told her.

"Okay. Be careful. I love you."

Carter froze.

There was a long—a very long—pause. Carter could almost hear Lacey regretting the slip.

She'd said it before. She hadn't been a bit shy about talking about love and what she wanted from him. But she hadn't said it casually like that, as if it was a normal part of their routine on the phone.

Carter was shocked by how much he wanted that routine.

Finally he cleared his throat.

"Oh my God, Carter, I'm sorry," she said in a rush. "I'm really not trying to push. It just came out. I—"

"Lacey," he said, low and firm.

She took a breath. "Yeah?"

"I love you, too."

There was another long pause and then he heard her sniff.

His heart clenched. "Lace—"

"I'm good," she said quickly, obviously knowing him well enough to know that her crying on the other end of the phone would be painful for him. She gave a little laugh. "I'm *so* good."

He relaxed. "Yeah?"

"Yeah. And now we *will* be meeting up behind the bleachers."

Her tone was teasing and happy and Carter realized once again what an aphrodisiac her happiness was.

What a sap.

But he was grinning as he shut his car off and got out as a carload of teens pulled into the parking lot. "I can't wait to see you."

"Me too."

They disconnected and Carter worked to get his mean cop face back into place before the kids saw him grinning like a fool.

———

The Renegades were pounding their rivals with only two minutes left until halftime.

Lacey surged to her feet with the rest of the crowd as the Renegades's quarterback drew his arm back and scanned the field. A moment later he saw his open man four yards from the goal line. He fired the ball in a tight spiral right into the running back's arms and the stands erupted as the kid sprinted into the end zone.

She felt Nolan's arms around her waist and a second later her feet left the ground as he lifted her, cheering loudly. She grinned and wrapped her arms around his neck.

She hadn't been a big football fan...before tonight. But an hour in the stands and she was already caught up in the excitement and the bond that brought everyone in Bad together on Friday nights in the fall. She could easily get used to the tailgating ahead of time and everyone gathering together in the stands, the palpable excited tension as the game started and the feeling of camaraderie that swept the crowd as the team succeeded and failed and succeeded again.

Nolan set her down and high-fived someone over her head while she scanned the crowd on the sidelines for Carter.

She saw him a second before he turned, also looking for her. Their eyes met and Lacey felt her grin spread as he pumped a fist into the air.

God he looked good happy.

Lacey had to admit that she'd seen his smile more and more over the past three weeks, but she'd been working to not get her hopes up. She'd love to think that she was a part of that, but it was happening fast and, frankly, she'd been pushy. She'd come to Bad unannounced and more or less forced him to take her in. She knew there were a lot of things about having her here that he liked. The almost constant sex-fest they had going on for one. He also liked her cooking and seemed to like just having her there at the end of the day. And in the morning. And when he managed to make it home for lunch in the middle of a shift.

Still, it had only been three weeks and he'd been honest and adamant about not being able to give her everything she wanted.

She felt a pang of sadness go through her followed swiftly by relief.

Earlier that day, for three minutes, she'd been going over and over everything Carter had said to her about forever and relationships and his father and what he did and didn't want. She'd also shifted over every touch, every smile, every sweet word he'd said.

She'd been almost convinced that it would all be okay, that Carter felt more than he was letting on. She knew he was scared but she knew he would come around and everything would be fine.

Then the timer had gone off and she'd looked at the pregnancy test. It had been negative. And none of the rest of it mattered.

"Hey, what's going on?"

Lacey blinked and looked around. She'd somehow reclaimed her seat next to Nolan without realizing it and she'd completely tuned out the game, the crowd and, evidently, whatever Nolan had just been saying.

The first half was over and the guys from the previous championship team had all started clearing out of the stands and making their way to the sidelines for the halftime ceremony.

She again searched for Carter and found him standing next to Jackson and Jase on the edge of the field.

"Lacey, are you okay?" Nolan asked, concern wrinkling his forehead.

She made herself smile and nod. "Yes, of course. Sorry. Spaced out for a second."

Just like she had for thirty minutes after seeing the confirmation that she was not pregnant. She'd sat on the bathroom floor, legs crisscrossed, the plastic stick with the one pink stripe on the tile in front of her, torn between relief—because really, that would have been a disaster—and sadness—because really, a child with Carter would have been…

"Maybe I should take you home," Nolan said, saving her from going down that particularly convoluted path.

Nolan knew she'd been sick. He'd brought her soup one day and he'd hung out and watched an *NCIS: Los Angeles* marathon with her one night while Carter worked. She knew Carter had sent him to check on her, but it had been sweet.

"I'm fine, really," she said. Okay, she was a little sick… evidently. She'd truly had herself talked into thinking it was morning sickness for a while. But it was obviously only a routine stomach bug instead. Big deal. That was a *relief*. She didn't want to feel that way for nine months. "I'm really feeling better," she told Nolan. And that was true. She'd started feeling better yesterday in fact. And had been disappointed about that.

Stupid, stupid, stupid. Being pregnant right now would have been so…complicated. She knew Carter was just now dealing with his feelings for her and just now coming around to thinking that maybe having her here permanently wasn't the end of the world.

She couldn't throw a baby in on top of that. Knowing what she did about Carter's past and his feelings about relationships, having him in a relationship with her because of a baby should have been the last thing she wanted. She totally understood where he was coming from when he said that he only wanted a relationship where everyone could walk away freely and easily and stayed because that was what they chose.

But she'd cried about the stupid pregnancy test anyway.

"Whoa, you're zoning out again," Nolan said, still frowning. "Come on." He took her elbow and pulled her to her feet.

"No, I want to stay," she insisted. "I'm sorry. I'm fine. Just a lot on my mind."

He studied her eyes, obviously not fully convinced. "Want to talk about it?"

"No, I—"

"Lacey, when I ask if you want to talk about it, what I really mean is you're *going to* talk about it or I'm taking you home. And *then* you're going to talk about it."

She opened her mouth to argue and then realized it was pointless. Nolan might seem like a laid-back guy but there was an alpha streak in him. Maybe it wasn't obvious on the surface, but she saw it in his eyes and heard it in his tone of voice. "Okay, fine. I'll tell you about it."

The moment the words left her mouth she realized she wanted to talk about it. She would love to bounce all of this off of someone else and for some reason she felt completely comfortable with Nolan.

"But you have to go down to the field and get your story first," she said, nudging him toward the steps that would lead them out of the stands. "Go do your thing and then we can talk after."

He let her push him to the steps but before he descended he turned. "Promise."

"Promise."

He took her hand and they left the bleachers together. Lacey went to the fence that separated the crowd from the field and Nolan made his way to the sidelines.

Carter and the other guys waited along the sideline as the announcer read their names one by one. Each one got cheers and applause and they were all grinning like they were sixteen again and obviously in their glory. When Carter's name was read, Lacey felt a surge of pride go through her and she clapped and yelled with the rest, watching him go down the line of former teammates and friends, fist bumping them and even guy-hugging a couple. At the end of the line stood Coach Karr, and Carter didn't hesitate before wrapping his arms around the man in a true hug…a father-son type of hug.

Lacey wished she could see his face. She felt tears sting her eyes.

Carter *did* know about family and about being there for people. Maybe his dad had made a mess of his relationships, but Carter had been surrounded by people who knew what it meant to love and support someone. Coach Karr had been there for all of the guys he coached. Even after he was done coaching them. And he'd taught them a lot more than just football. It was why they were all here tonight in the first place—to honor a man who had been not just a pillar of the community and the football program, but who had given his players something every kid needed. Unconditional love.

Carter *did* know how to do that, how to be there for someone. He just had to stop being scared.

When all of the players had been introduced and Coach had greeted each of them individually, his daughter, Elyse, walked with him to the center of the field where the superintendent and high school principal waited.

The announcer read the long list of Coach's accomplishments and then they directed everyone's attention to the press box. A large white sheet was hanging over the concession stand and, at the principal's command, the sheet fell away to reveal a new sign.

The stadium would now be known as the Davis Karr Stadium.

Lacey blinked against the tears that threatened when she saw Coach Karr's face, and then when she looked at Carter and saw the same emotion in his expression, she felt a tear slip down her cheek.

She'd never met Coach Karr in person but she was grateful to him for loving Carter.

The rest of the ceremony went quickly as the halftime clock ticked down and soon all of the guys were leaving the field. Carter came past and caught her up in a big hug and spun her around.

"Is it time to make out behind the bleachers?" she asked, laughing. God, she loved seeing him happy.

"I wish." Carter set her back on her feet. "I gotta go flush the parking lot of underage drinkers and then there are some Autre alums down at Bad Brews. I need to go be sure no one starts running their mouth as the game winds down."

She lifted onto tiptoe and pressed a kiss to his lips. "Okay. I'll see you at the party?"

He grimaced.

"No?" Dang, she'd been looking forward to relaxing with him. Maybe dancing a bit. Maybe sneaking off to a quiet corner.

"Eventually, yes," he said. "But it might take some time to get everything settled down after the game."

"Hey guys."

Lacey glanced over at Nolan. She grinned. "You looked as excited as the rest of them out there."

"Just thinking of the website hits I'm going to get on my story. Readers eat this stuff up," he said with a wink.

"Hey, Nolan, can you take Lacey to the after party?" Carter asked. "I can meet you guys there."

"Yeah. You up to it?" Nolan asked Lacey.

She rolled her eyes but not before Carter jumped on the question.

"You're not feeling good again? Maybe you should go home and rest."

"I'm *fine*," she told them both. "I promise I will tell you if that changes."

"Well, you also promised to tell me what was going on earlier in the stands. You ready to talk?" Nolan asked.

Lacey wanted to slug him. He should know better than to bring something like that up in front of Carter, because Carter would—

"What happened in the stands?" Carter moved in closer to her, cupping her face and searching her eyes.

She sighed. "Nothing."

"She's just a little out of it tonight," Nolan said.

Damn him.

She frowned at him and then gave Carter a big, reassuring smile. "I'm fine."

But Carter was focused on Nolan. "What does 'out of it' mean?"

"She's a little spacey or something."

"I'm right *here*," she reminded them. She grasped Carter's hand. "I'm fine. It's nothing. Still resting up from being sick. But I'm fine."

"Maybe you should—"

She grabbed Nolan's hand too. "Nolan will be right with me all night. If I'm not fine, I promise to tell him and let him take me home, okay?"

Carter gritted his teeth and looked at the other man. "You'll take care of her?"

"Of course."

He sighed, clearly not entirely happy, but he couldn't *make* her go home. "Okay. I'll get there as soon as I can."

Thank God. She breathed and smiled. "I can't wait."

Carter leaned in and kissed her cheek, gave Nolan one last pointed look and then turned to head for the parking lot.

Nolan waited until Carter was out of sight, then he grasped her elbow and steered her behind the bleachers.

This wasn't exactly how she'd envisioned the stolen moments behind the stands during the game.

Nolan let go of her and crossed his arms. "Okay, spill."

Fine. If he was going to be insistent and stubborn and bossy, she'd tell him.

"I took a pregnancy test today."

His arms dropped. "Oh."

She smiled at the fact that it was obvious he had no idea what to say. "It was negative."

Nolan nodded. "Oh."

"And I'm bouncing between being glad and realizing that would have been a huge complication, and feeling…sad."

Nolan hesitated for a moment, then reached out and put his hand against her cheek. "Sorry."

She felt the stupid sadness drift over her but shook her head. "No, it's good. I mean, God, Carter would freak out."

Nolan pressed his lips together and she felt her chest tighten. Nolan agreed that it would be a bad thing for her and Carter. Damn.

She knew it. Of course she did. But she hated having it confirmed.

She sighed and turned away. "I know it would be a bad thing. I know that the last thing Carter needs is to feel trapped. But at the same time…" She pulled in a deep breath. "Part of me wants to trap him."

Nolan gave a bark of laughter. "Probably shouldn't put it quite that way."

She turned with a smile. "I know. I don't mean it. Exactly. I guess I want *him* to want that. Even if it's not now. Someday. You know?"

Nolan nodded. "I do. But, honey, I don't want you to get hurt. Carter is…Carter."

"Yeah. I know." She did. She knew it. And it wasn't fair for her to want to change things when he'd been so honest about everything.

"I'm not saying that a part of him doesn't want all of that," Nolan said after a moment. "I think maybe he does with you. He loves you, Lacey."

She nodded. "I know."

"If anyone could change his mind it would be you. But, really, I don't think you should expect anything."

It was so stupid. She knew all of this. *Knew it.* Had always known it.

"Garrett thought we could have a long-term threesome."

She wasn't sure where the words came from but she had so many emotions swirling around, it felt as if she couldn't keep them inside any longer.

Nolan didn't look shocked. "Carter mentioned something about it."

That shocked *her.* "He did?"

Nolan nodded. "And he mentioned that he felt like Garrett balanced him out."

"I don't know what to do. Carter's been completely honest with me about everything. And I really thought I was fine…until I started wondering if I was pregnant. And then I started hoping. And then when the test was negative…" She dashed away a tear that sprang up suddenly. "And I realized I do want that. All of it."

Nolan stepped forward and folded her in his arms. She wrapped her arms around his waist. The hug felt good. Comforting. He rested his chin on top of her head.

After a moment he said, "You have to tell him."

"That I want a baby?"

"Yes."

She swallowed hard. "We've only been together for three weeks."

Nolan chuckled, the sound rumbling against her ear, making her feel calmer. "You've been together a hell of a lot longer than that, Lacey."

"I don't want to lose him. He doesn't want to tie me down. And I understand. Kind of. I guess."

"I'm not sure Carter totally understands it either," Nolan said. "If that's any consolation."

It wasn't. At all.

"And I was hoping it would be an accident and then he wouldn't have a choice," she admitted.

Nolan leaned back and looked down at her. "You know that's not fair."

"I know."

"Talk to him."

She nodded. "Okay."

"Sooner versus later," Nolan added.

"Okay."

"Like tonight."

She frowned at him. "*Okay.*"

He hugged her again. "He loves you, Lacey. Just remember that."

Yeah, she would remember that. But she also remembered that he'd loved her the last time he'd walked away when he found out she wanted something he didn't.

CHAPTER
TEN

SHE WAS PREGNANT.

Carter sat on the edge of the tub staring at the white plastic stick with the pink line that said he was going to be a father.

Holy shit.

A *father.*

Pregnant.

He and Lacey were going to have a baby. A child. They were going to bring a life into the world. Together. For the next eighteen years they were going to be making decisions together. Ideally, they would *be* together for the next eighteen years. Or longer. Everyone knew that parenthood didn't end after eighteen years.

He was going to be a father. He was going to have to teach someone else how to throw a ball and ride a bike and drive a car and balance a checkbook. He was going to have to have words of wisdom. He was going to have to teach someone else how to be a good person.

Carter forced the words through his mind. He tried to focus on them. He wanted them to hit him square in the chest. He wanted to feel the wave of panic. He wanted to catalog all of the reasons this was a terrible thing.

But all he felt was possessiveness and protectiveness. And a definite touch of happiness.

Lacey was going to have his baby.

There was going to be a *person* in the world that was half him and half Lacey.

And because of that person, Lacey was going to be bound to him for the next eighteen plus years.

There was nothing panicking about that. That sounded damned good, in fact.

And *that* was what panicked him.

One of his first thoughts was that Lacey was now stuck and he was happy about it.

Yeah, that wasn't good.

Carter got to his feet, grabbed the plastic stick and headed for the door.

He'd come home to change clothes before heading to the party at Bad Memories. He'd come into the bathroom to brush his teeth and had seen that Mooch had knocked the trashcan over. In gathering up the trash, he'd seen the stick.

He'd never seen one in person before but he knew what it was. And he knew what that line meant.

He drove to Coach's without really focusing on the road. He was still in uniform, the pregnancy test in his pocket, but all he could think about was that he needed to see Lacey *now*.

She couldn't have told him before this. If she'd taken the test that afternoon, she'd only known for a few hours, and during the football game, while he was on duty, wasn't the ideal time to talk about all of this.

He wasn't upset she hadn't told him. He just needed to see her. He needed to hug her and bury his nose in her hair and tell her that he loved her and…somehow convince them both that he wasn't going to fuck everything up.

Carter parked his truck at the back of the huge cluster of cars and trucks on the gravel and grass in front of the community center. The front doors were thrown open and light, music, and laughter spilled out into the night.

Tables of food were set up near the bar and it looked like Jase, Priscilla, Marc, Luke, and Bailey were all helping to bartend tonight, and they were hopping at the moment. Marc's fiancé, Sabrina, was on stage singing with her band The Locals, for the couples moving over the wooden floorboards of the dancefloor.

Carter honed in on Lacey like she wore a tracking device.

She was dancing with Nolan—snug up against him, in fact.

Carter frowned. It was Nolan. Carter had absolutely no reason to be worried or jealous. Lacey loved *him*, he knew that. What surprised him wasn't the lack of jealousy but the feeling of *thank God* that went through him.

Seeing Nolan there made Carter breathe easier. He had no idea what he was going to say to Lacey, but he couldn't get too crazy without Nolan intervening. He'd promised as much at the coffee shop. Nolan would keep Carter from doing anything stupid.

Carter headed straight for them. He was vaguely aware of people greeting him as he moved past, but he didn't spare so much as a glance around.

"Lacey."

She pulled back and looked over at him. Her face relaxed into a smile immediately. "Hey."

But Carter couldn't seem to pull his own face out of the tight, pinched frown. "We need to talk."

Her eyes widened. "We do?"

"Everything okay?" It was Nolan who asked.

Carter finally looked at his friend. Nolan looked concerned and hadn't yet let go of Lacey.

"Hope so," Carter said truthfully.

One of Nolan's eyebrows went up. Clearly he read something in Carter's voice or face.

"Carter, what's going on?" Lacey asked.

He looked at her. "I want to get married."

She froze. And stared at him. Her mouth moved but nothing came out.

Nolan stepped closer to her again. "Lace?"

Carter wanted to growl at him but Lacey gave Nolan a smile that hit Carter in the gut. He liked that smile. He knew he was being intense but he couldn't help it. Things were swirling through him so fast that he couldn't think straight. He was going on almost pure emotion here. Nolan would balance that out.

"I'm okay," she told him.

Nolan's stance relaxed but he was watching Carter carefully. "Maybe we should go outside."

Not "maybe *you* should go outside" but "*we*".

Carter made himself breathe deeply. Then he stepped closer to Lacey and took her face between his hands. "Marry me."

"But...wha... I..."

She looked as perplexed as she sounded and Carter felt a shot of dread go through him. He wanted her. Forever. And now she *had* to marry him. She was pregnant.

But he had to resist the urge to say that out loud. Because then he really would sound like his dad.

"Carter," Nolan said, low and even. "Outside."

His tone was firm and he had a hand on Lacey's lower back and a hand on Carter's shoulder. Okay. Outside. Probably a good idea.

Carter glanced around as he turned. Not *everyone's* attention was on them but the couples closest to them were definitely watching with interest.

Dammit.

Carter snagged Lacey's hand and pulled her along with him as he let Nolan's more rational mind take the lead. When they hit the doorway and the breeze touched his face, Carter dragged in some oxygen. He felt some tension leave his shoulders as Nolan led them around to the back of the building. It was dark back here. They could still easily hear the music and low hum of conversation from the party, but here it was just the three of them.

They came to a stop and Carter concentrated on Lacey. "I love you, Lace. I want you forever and you deserve it all— marriage, kids, the whole thing. Marry me. Please."

She frowned. "Are you drunk? What's going on?"

Okay, it was out of the blue. He'd give her that.

"Of course I'm not drunk." He felt a little drunk. Crazy. Out of control. But he hadn't had a drop.

"This is all really sudden," she said.

Yes, in the overall scheme of things, fertilization of an egg did happen suddenly.

"Is it sudden?" Carter asked. "Really?" And she wasn't going to tell him about the baby *now*? But maybe she didn't want to talk about it in front of Nolan. "I've loved you for two years. We've been through a lot. Things have always been so mixed up, but now I really think we can make it simple. Marry me."

It was like someone had possessed him. Of course a baby didn't have to mean marriage. They didn't *have* to get married. They didn't even have to live together. He would be involved, he'd help her out however he could, but making a commitment to their child didn't mean they had to make a legal, binding, forever commitment to one another.

But he wanted that. And this was the perfect reason. It didn't make him *crazy* to want this…*this* made sense.

"You don't want to get married," she reminded him.

"I changed my mind."

Because the baby was the perfect excuse to keep Lacey in his life even when he said and did stupid things. Lacey would love a baby to the depths of her soul and wouldn't let anything keep her from being with her child. Not even the child's dumbass father.

"I want to," she finally said, looking into his eyes. "I want to marry you, Carter. I love you. But I have to be sure that you're *sure.*"

He started to say that of course he was sure, that he'd do anything to make her happy, that this was meant to be, but at the last moment he heard his father's voice…saying those same things.

This panic over possibly losing her—was this how his father felt? Was this how Matt felt when he kept pushing until he drove them away?

"I have no idea if I'm sure, Lace. I feel sure right now. But I'm probably not going to be good at it."

Carter thought that was positive—that he could admit that he didn't really know what he was doing. His father never admitted that.

"I think I'll leave you two alone," Nolan said.

"No!"

Carter reached out and grabbed the other man's arm. He needed someone to make sure he was proposing romantically and giving her the option of saying no and *not* throwing her over his shoulder and finding the nearest aisle.

Nolan was clearly surprised. "Carter—"

"Just…don't go yet."

He needed someone to keep him in check.

Nolan frowned but after looking into Carter's eyes he gave a single nod. "Fine."

Carter felt relief wash through him. Okay, he wasn't going to do anything stupid as long as Nolan was there. Carter looked at Lacey. "Let's go home. Let's just talk about everything."

They were going to talk about the baby. He wouldn't force her to marry him but if there was a child in the equation, it did change some things. He just wanted to hear her say that.

Lacey glanced at Nolan. "I thought—"

"Nolan will come too." Carter felt his friend's questioning look but he didn't meet Nolan's eyes. "Please, Lace."

Lacey took a deep breath. "Okay."

Maybe she sensed that they needed Nolan there too.

"I, uh…" Nolan glanced back at the front of the community center as Carter grabbed Lacey's hand and started for his truck.

"Come on, Winters, you'd do anything for Lacey, right?"

Nolan frowned but nodded. "Yeah, okay." He walked behind them into the parking area, but then pointed at his own car. "I'll follow you."

Carter and Lacey didn't talk for the first few miles, but finally Carter couldn't take it.

"I want you to know that I'm really happy." He gripped the steering wheel tightly.

"Me too. But are you sure you're okay?" she asked.

Her expression was worried when he looked at her. "I'm reeling a little, but I'm getting used to the idea already," he said simply.

She pivoted on the seat. "You're already getting used to the idea of being engaged?"

"Well, yeah, that too."

"Too?"

He glanced over again. "You want to do this at home?"

"Do what?"

He frowned and looked back to the road. "Talk about the baby."

There was a long pause.

"The baby?" she finally asked softly.

"I found the pregnancy test."

"Oh."

He looked over. "Oh?"

"I just…dammit, did I not throw it away?"

"Mooch dug through the trash. You're upset that I know?"

She sighed. "There's nothing to know. The test was negative."

"It was—" He braked and pulled over on the side of the road. He slammed the truck into park. He turned to look at her. "It was *negative*?"

"Yes. You didn't notice that?"

"How the hell was I supposed to *notice* that?"

"There was only one line."

He stared at her. "How many lines are there supposed to be?"

"Two. If you're pregnant."

He let that sink in. "There was only one."

"Right."

"So…no baby."

She pressed her lips together and shook her head. "No baby."

"Oh."

They sat without talking for almost a minute. The silence was broken by the sound of Nolan knocking on Carter's window.

Carter rolled it down. "Hey."

"You guys okay? What's going on?"

What was going on was that he had lost the best and biggest reason for Lacey to stay with him forever. That was all Carter could think about.

"He found the test," Lacey said when Carter failed to respond. "He thought it was positive."

"Ah."

"Wait a second." Carter looked from Lacey to Nolan. "You knew about the test?"

"Lacey told me at the game."

Carter swung to face Lacey. "You told *him*? Why?"

Her eyes were wide. "I was…conflicted. I needed someone to talk to."

"This is why you were out of it at the game," Carter said, the pieces coming together.

"I was distracted. Nolan noticed."

Carter looked back to his friend. And even more pieces clicked.

Nolan was the person Lacey had turned to. Nolan had been there for her. He'd been there for Carter too. He'd calmed the situation, supported them both.

Carter faced forward and put the truck into gear. "Let's go home."

Nolan stepped back from the side of the truck. "So you guys are good?"

"I'll see you at my place," Carter told him.

"Uh…" Nolan finally nodded. "Okay."

Carter pulled back onto the road. They were only about a mile from his drive.

"Carter, I didn't turn to Nolan instead of you. He was just there and—"

"Lace, it's fine," Carter interrupted. "It's good. I'm glad he was there for you."

They were quiet until he turned onto the street that would lead to his house.

"You only proposed because of the baby," she said.

He wasn't going to lie to her. "I proposed because thinking you were pregnant helped me realize that I do want to have you here with me forever." He pulled up in front of the house and killed the engine. He turned to look at her. "I want to do the marriage and kids thing with you, Lacey. But I'm going to fuck it up."

She shook her head. Her eyes sparkled with tears in the light coming through the windows from the tall yard lamp. "You won't. Just love me."

"I do. And I'll do *whatever* it takes to make sure you're happy and have what you need."

Nolan pulled up behind them and Carter took a deep breath. He knew exactly what he had to do.

"I love you, Lacey," he said. "I want you to know that."

"I do."

Carter opened his door and got out. He rounded the truck and took her hand as she slid to the ground. Nolan came up the driveway behind Carter's truck.

"Let's go inside," Carter said simply. "I don't know about you guys, but I could use a drink." He led them into the kitchen.

"I'm going to run upstairs and change my clothes," Lacey said.

For the first time, Carter really took in her appearance. She was wearing jeans, a Renegades t-shirt, and had her hair up in a ponytail. She looked like…a small town football fan.

"You look amazing," he said. He glanced at Nolan. "Doesn't she?"

Nolan looked surprised but he turned to look at Lacey. "She does. Of course."

She gave them both a smile and then headed for the stairs.

Carter moved to the fridge and grabbed two bottles of beer as he waited for Lacey to get out of earshot. But the moment he heard the bedroom door shut, he said, "Do you remember the time I saved your ass from getting beat up after school?"

Nolan took one of the bottles when Carter held it out. "You mean when we were *eight*?"

"So you do remember."

Nolan twisted the cap off his beer. "Okay, I remember."

"So I'm gonna need you to pay it back tonight."

Nolan sighed and took a drink. "I don't want to hear this, do I?" he asked after he'd swallowed.

"We're going to have to make out."

Nolan scratched his jaw. "I'll give you a kidney or something. I'm not kissing you, Carter."

Carter sighed. "With *Lacey*. You owe me."

"That's a terrible idea," Nolan said evenly. He took another drink and narrowed his eyes. "What the hell is going on?"

"It's for Lacey."

"For Lacey?"

"I have to show her that I'm willing to do it this time."

"Make out with another guy?"

"Share her."

Nolan was quiet for a moment. "You think that's what Lacey wants?"

Carter drew a breath in through his nose and let it out. "It's what she needs."

"She *needs* to have sex with two guys?"

"No." Carter scowled at Nolan. "She needs to be loved and taken care of by two guys."

"Carter," Nolan said slowly. "I don't want you to take this the wrong way, but I'm not in love with Lacey."

"You will be," he said with a frown. "Give it like five minutes. That's how long it took me," he added with a mutter.

Nolan smiled at that. "You love her enough for two guys."

Carter shook his head. "That's not the point. The point is, she wants to be married and have kids and stuff."

"Yes, with *you*."

"But *I* am obsessed with her. I need someone to help balance things out. I need someone to keep me from freaking out. I need someone like you." He couldn't look at Nolan as he said it.

Nolan didn't reply for a long minute. Carter took two healthy swigs of his beer and waited. Nolan was the rational one here. He was the reasonable one. He wasn't in love with Lacey but that was a *good* thing. He would help Carter stay objective. Nolan cared about her. He had been concerned when she'd been sick for the past several days and he'd been there for her when she'd been upset earlier tonight. That was enough. Carter did love her enough for two men. He just needed someone else to care about her enough to keep *him* from making her miserable.

"So how would this work exactly?" Nolan finally asked.

Carter's head came up quickly and he stared at the other man. "You'd consider it?"

Nolan shrugged. "I don't know. Tell me the logistics."

"The logistics?"

"Yeah. How it would work. I'd have to commute to San Antonio some of the time for work but I could do some of it remotely. I do travel a lot."

Carter frowned. "Okay." What the hell did that have to do with anything?

"So do I get my own bedroom here or do you have enough closet space in your bedroom for all our stuff? And do you guys get to have sex when I'm not here? Because that would mean that Lacey and I could have sex when you're working a night shift, I guess."

Carter felt his hand tighten on his beer bottle. "No sex when I'm not here."

"So no sex when *I'm* not here," Nolan said, nodding. "That's fair I guess."

"I will have sex with Lacey whenever I want to."

Nolan frowned. "So, do I still get to date other women?"

"Lacey your first priority."

"That's not a no."

"I...fuck, Nolan, I don't know." How did this shit work? Was there any way to keep jealousy out of the equation? Because the thought of Lacey and Nolan together alone...or hell, even with Carter *there*...made him want to punch someone.

No, not someone. Nolan. It made him want to punch Nolan.

Nolan lifted his bottle to his lips. Carter watched him. He seemed pretty casual about this whole thing.

Strangely casual.

"Are you bisexual?" Carter asked.

Nolan choked on his swallow of beer. He coughed for a moment. Then he gave Carter a level look. "No. Not even a little. Sorry."

"Fuck your sorry. I don't want you, man," Carter said.

Nolan gave him a grin. "Just making sure we're on the same page. Buck naked in the bedroom is probably not the time to have these discussions, you know?"

Yeah, he knew. He definitely knew.

"This would be purely about Lacey. Sharing her." Carter almost choked on the last two words.

"Okay. So how does that work? I mean, exactly?" Nolan asked. "I'm not quite the worldly playboy that you are. Do we take her at the same time—and if so, I'm gonna need a tutorial on that one. I mean I get the basic idea but haven't been there, you know? Or do we go one after another? And if it's one after another, do we flip a coin to see who goes first?"

Carter gritted his teeth and squeezed his bottle again.

Part of him really thought Nolan was messing with him, but damn. He just couldn't get past the urge to rip Nolan's head off for even *talking* about all of this. All of this that *Carter* had brought up.

Further proof that he was completely irrational when it came to Lacey.

"It'll depend on what Lacey wants," Carter managed to say. Somehow.

"Do we talk it all out ahead of time or is it a heat-of-the-moment thing?" Nolan asked. "And what if she wants us to touch each other? Then you're cool with it?"

It hit Carter that he didn't really know what Lacey might ask for in the heat of the moment.

"You know I'm talking about more than sex, right?" Carter asked. *That* was the key here. Nolan had to pick up the emotional stuff Carter was going to screw up. "I want you to be her friend, to support her, to help her understand that I love her even when I don't do a good job of showing it. Make her laugh, be romantic, be fun."

Nolan seemed to think all of that over. "And what do *you* do then?"

"I…" Love her more than anyone else ever would. "Do everything else."

Thank God Lacey made her reappearance just then. She was dressed in light cotton capris and a top with spaghetti straps that hugged her body. She'd brushed her hair out and had washed her makeup off. She gave them a big smile and crossed to the fridge, where she grabbed a beer. She turned to face them as she twisted the top off and sighed. "The party was fun but I'd always rather relax at home."

"You look absolutely beautiful," Nolan told her, crossing the tile floor to where she stood.

Carter felt his whole body tighten and grow cold. But he forced himself to stay where he was.

"Uh." Lacey's gaze flickered to Carter, then back to Nolan. "Thanks."

Nolan moved in front of her, blocking her from Carter.

And delivered on the favor Carter had just asked of him.

CHAPTER
ELEVEN

"TRUST ME," Nolan whispered.

Then he cupped the back of Lacey's head and pulled her in for a kiss.

A *kiss*.

With Carter standing across the kitchen.

Any other woman might have protested, out of shock or confusion. But Lacey wasn't shocked or confused at all. At least not after the first three seconds. Because she knew the man she loved very well.

Carter thought they needed Nolan.

Dammit.

If it wasn't for the "trust me" from Nolan, she would have pushed him back and demanded to know what was going on. But after those first three seconds, she thought *what the hell* and decided to kiss him back.

He wasn't Carter. He would never be Carter. But he was a good kisser. And no doubt all of this was Carter's idea.

She let Nolan lead her into a deeper kiss. He urged her mouth open and slid his tongue over her bottom lip then along her tongue. She met the erotic slide with her own for a few strokes.

When he let her lips go, he trailed his mouth along her jaw to her ear. "He has to be the one to stop it," he said quietly.

She took a breath. Then tipped her head to the side, giving him more access to her neck.

Nolan kissed along her collarbone and she had to fight to keep her gaze from finding Carter. She closed her eyes instead.

Carter thought he couldn't give her everything she needed. He was probably thinking he was bringing Nolan into their relationship for her. But the truth was, it was for *him*. He could hide behind Nolan. If there was someone else to take up the slack, he wouldn't have to try as hard. He'd been living with her for three weeks, he'd thought he was going to be stuck with her because of a baby, and he'd realized that there were parts to a relationship that he wasn't prepared for. The parts that Garrett had always done. Carter didn't even *know* about some of the hard parts of a relationship. When had he ever been in a serious relationship? Never. Except with her and Garrett. Now he thought could do the parts he liked and let Nolan do the rest.

Well, *that* was bullshit.

With that thought, she wrapped her arms around Nolan's neck, arched against him and took his mouth in a full-on hot, wet kiss.

She felt the strap of her shirt slide off her shoulder and Nolan's hand on her breast.

Then she felt Nolan being jerked away from her.

Carter stood between them, scowling. Nolan caught her eye and then ran his thumb over his bottom lip. She sighed and pulled her strap back up.

"Fuck, I can't do it."

Nolan nodded at Carter's words. "You lasted two minutes longer than I thought you would."

Carter looked pissed, but she wasn't so sure that he was pissed at Nolan. Or her. The anger seemed very self-directed.

"What the hell were you thinking?" she asked Carter. "Seriously."

Carter shoved Nolan back farther and then turned to face her, firmly between the two of them. "I was thinking that I would do anything to make a relationship with you work. But I can't."

"You can't let another guy fuck me? Well, that's great, Carter. We've really come a long way," she said. Yes, she was angry. Because Carter was trying to take the easy way out.

Again.

She was worth more than that. She was worth some freaking *emotion*. He'd let Garrett handle all of that stuff. She and Carter had always had fantastic conversations. They'd laughed. They'd had hot, amazing, consuming sex. They had a lot of similar interests. But she'd never cried on his shoulder. They'd never fought.

"A year ago I was sharing you," he said with a scowl. "I'd say this is different."

"You were sharing me because you were too afraid to actually try having a relationship with me the very first night we met."

"Because I knew I wasn't good enough for you."

"At least your father *tries*."

There was a long horrible moment of silence. Nobody moved. Lacey was sure she didn't even breathe.

Carter backed up a step. "What does that mean?"

"Your dad sucks at relationships," Lacey said. "But he keeps trying. He knows they might leave. Statistically, it's practically a given. But he keeps going after what he wants."

"My dad doesn't know what he's doing!" Carter shoved a hand through his hair and then scrubbed the back of his neck, clearly agitated.

"But he does," Lacey said. She took a breath and pushed her shoulders back and met his gaze. "He knows how to love someone. He's always loved *you*. And *you* know how to love— you've got Coach and Nolan and Jackson and the other guys. And you had Garrett. You know all about love. You're just scared."

"Of hurting you, yes," he said.

"That's funny, because the only times you've hurt me have been the times when you *haven't* tried to love me."

Carter stared at her for several heartbeats and Lacey made herself stand straight and still until he made a decision.

"You should go."

His words were soft, but they were firm and his gaze met hers directly as he said them.

Lacey felt as if he'd slapped her, but she fought not to show it.

"Carter—" Nolan started.

"*No.*" Carter kept his eyes on Lacey. "You *have to* go."

She pressed her lips together. So he wasn't going to try. He wasn't even going to give her a good fight. He was just going to give up because things got a little tough.

She took a deep breath and then made herself walk past him. "I'll get my stuff."

She had no idea where she was going to go. She supposed that she could crash on Nolan's couch. Or there was a bed-and-breakfast in town. Or maybe Annabelle and Jackson had a spare room.

But she wasn't leaving Bad.

Because as she walked past Carter and caught his scent and everything in her clenched with need and love, she realized that he did need her to go.

He needed to know that he would give her a choice. He needed to know he could *let* her go.

He needed to know he wasn't his father.

That was fine.

But he was also going to find out that she wasn't like his stepmothers. She wasn't going to leave just because he was being a jackass.

Ten minutes later, her suitcase was in the back of Nolan's car and they were headed for the motel.

"You can stay with me," Nolan said for the fourth time. "He's going to come around."

"It's going to take a while," she said, resigned to waiting the stubborn ass out. "And I don't think staying with you is the best choice."

"Well, it would be staying with my mom," Nolan said with a smile. "Like I am. There's a guest room and my mom is an excellent cook."

Lacey felt some of the dark mood lift. "You know, you really are a good guy to have around."

Nolan gave her a look. "Yeah, it's called friendship, and I'm not going anywhere either. I mean, I'm going back to San Antonio eventually, but I'll always be there for you. For both of you."

In that moment, Lacey decided that she was going to find a Bad girl for Nolan. She'd love to have him around more.

"So you realize that he's got to learn that not everyone leaves too?" Lacey said.

"He does. And he has to realize that not wanting to share you is normal. Just because Garrett was into it and Carter isn't, doesn't mean Carter is wrong."

Nolan's words rocked through her. He was right. Completely right.

"And," Nolan added. "Just like Carter has to step into Garrett's shoes for you in a lot of ways...you have to do the same for him."

She sat up in the seat. That had never occurred to her. "You're right. He's missing his best friend."

Nolan smiled and reached over to squeeze her knee. "No, she's right here. But her feelings are hurt because *her* best friend is being kind of a dumbass."

She couldn't believe it, but she laughed at that.

Maybe it wasn't love that Carter needed to learn about, but unconditional friendship.

Lacey sat back in the seat with a smile and wrapped her arms around herself. She felt lighter. Carter had a ways to go, but he'd get there. Garrett had loved Carter through a lot of dumbass moments, she was sure. She could do the same.

———

"Well, you look like hell."

Carter gave Bailey, the bartender at Bad Brews, a bland look. "Your flirting could use some work."

She laughed. "When I flirt with you, Officer Shaw, you'll know it."

He studied her. She was never going to flirt with him. She was madly in love with Luke Hamilton. And Carter realized they were perfect together. How had he and all of their friends missed that all the years they'd known them both?

"Well, then your pep talks could use some work," he told her.

She grinned. "Not really my expertise."

"You're a bartender. Isn't that part of the code or something?"

Bailey set a shot glass on the bar and filled it with tequila. "Here's the code—pour drinks and listen. If you need either of those things, I'm your girl."

Carter opened his mouth to say something flirtatious, or even outright offensive, about her being his girl but nothing came out. His mind spun with possibilities but he found he didn't want to say any of them.

What the hell?

But he knew.

Lacey.

She had taken away his ability to be inappropriate with other women. Even women who expected it.

Dammit.

It had been three days since she'd gone back to Baton Rouge and he'd been a miserable prick every minute of those three days. And there were no signs of that improving anytime soon.

Bailey cocked an eyebrow. "Wow, she does have your panties in a wad."

Carter shot back the tequila and frowned at her. "Being in love sucks."

She refilled his shot glass. "Everyone knows that, Carter."

He shot that one back too, welcoming the burn down his throat to his gut and hoping that the fuzziness the liquor would cause in his brain would start soon. "No, that isn't even true," he said after he'd swallowed. "It doesn't suck. I just suck."

Bailey tipped her head. "What did you do?"

He tapped the edge of the shot glass. She looked like she wasn't sure she should refill it again, but she did.

"It's not what I did," he said. "It's what I *didn't* do." He took the shot and downed it.

"What *didn't* you do?"

"I didn't marry Kristina Martin," he said, finally feeling the tequila haze start to settle around his thoughts. "I should have. She was smart and sweet and pretty."

Bailey looked mildly amused as she leaned in on her elbows on the bar. "You should have married Kristina Martin?"

"Definitely," he agreed. "Absolutely."

"But you didn't want to get married. To anyone," Bailey said.

"But now I do," Carter said.

The corner of Bailey's mouth kicked up. "Kristina Martin?"

Carter leaned in. "Well, that would be perfect. Except that I'm madly in love with Lacey and that's probably not going to make Kristina very happy."

"A proposal from you might make Kristina's husband a little unhappy too," Bailey said dryly.

"Right. It's a big mess."

But he'd let her leave, Carter reminded himself. He'd *made* her leave, even. He should be feeling proud of that.

But he wasn't. At all. He was feeling miserable and for the past three days he'd been constantly one second away from driving to Baton Rouge and carrying her off to the nearest Justice of the Peace.

Nolan was supposed to have kept him in check, he was

supposed to have helped him, but instead he'd pushed Carter to the point of snapping. Nolan had kissed Lacey—and dammit, Lacey had kissed him back—and Carter had thrown them both out.

That was kind of the opposite of what he'd been going for.

"Listen, if you're going to keep shooting tequila like it's the answer to all your problems, I'm going to need to know who to call for you later and I'm going to ask you to move your sorry, pathetic ass over to the sorry, pathetic table." She pointed behind him. "I don't want you depressing everyone else who comes in here tonight."

Carter swiveled to look for the table she was talking about.

JD Evans sat across the room at a round table near the back door. He had a nearly empty pitcher of beer and two completely empty shot glasses in front of him.

Carter knew JD. He was a firefighter and EMT over in Autre. Not only had they had reasons to work together before as first responders—a few car accidents, a couple of fires, and a missing person—JD came to Bad to drink and hang out a few times with their fire chief, Michael LeClaire. They were nice guys, and great at their jobs. Carter liked having the Autre guys on his side when it came to shit that required his badge. That included their cop, Zander Landry as well. Not that Carter would ever admit that to his old football teammates, who had played against Landry and *all* his brothers and cousins. But LeClaire had been a few years older and JD wasn't from Louisiana so they got a pass.

And right now JD looked like Carter felt.

"Yeah, okay." Carter took the two beers Bailey slid across the bar to him and headed to JD's table. "Hey."

"Hey, Carter."

"Bailey said I had to move it over here. I'm bringing her down."

"That right?" JD looked past him to the bar. "Well, I try not to argue with pretty bartenders. Or really anyone willing to pour me beer."

Carter chuckled. "Good policy." He slid into the seat across from JD. "What's up with you?"

"A woman," JD said, lifting his glass to his lips. He drank and swallowed. "What's wrong with you?"

"Same."

They sat in companionable silence for nearly a minute, each thinking about his own issues. Then Carter had to ask, "Someone I know?"

"Yep." But JD didn't elaborate.

Okay.

Carter drank down half his beer and wished he'd brought more shots over with him.

"What are you drinkin'?" Carter asked.

"PBR." JD slid his pitcher closer to his side of the table. "Pitchers are on sale. I'm not sharing."

Carter grimaced. "PBR? You *are* having a shitty day."

"You have no idea."

Carter tipped his beer and drained the bottle before setting it down. "Bet I can top you."

Bailey set four more shots of tequila on the table just then. "Looks like y'all might need these."

JD grinned up at her. "Thanks, Bay, you're the best."

"The *best*," Carter agreed, picking up one of the glasses.

She smirked. "Yeah, I'm a regular humanitarian."

Carter clinked his glass against JD's and shot the liquor back.

It barely burned this time. A good sign.

"Okay, you want this next shot, you have to tell me why you deserve it," JD said, pointing to the two remaining glasses.

Carter frowned. "I have to deserve it?"

"Yep. Two shots to the guy with the worst day."

"Okay." He'd play. "I'm in love. She loves me too. But *I* am the type of guy to be so in love that I'll eventually make the other person miserable. So, because I love her, I realized that I needed to push her away. Which I did. And...it worked. She's gone."

JD just stared at him for a long moment.

"What?" Carter finally asked.

"You're a dumbass. But I'm totally getting both shots."

Carter scowled. "Hey."

"No, seriously. The woman you love, loves you too. Wants to be with you. And *you* pushed *her* away and now you're down here miserable, pissed, and getting shit-faced because you *got your way*? Dude..."

"Fine. Let's hear why you're down here miserable and pissed and getting shit-faced."

"Okay. I fell in love, she did too, I fucked it up by being a selfish prick, she told me to come find her when I got my shit together, I got my shit partially together, packed up my life in Omaha, moved all the way down here to a fuckin' *swamp*, decided I didn't have my life *enough* together, avoided her, then just when I thought maybe I was ready after all, found out that she's in love with someone else. Someone way better than me, no matter how much shit I get together. So I waited too long and lost her."

Carter arched a brow. "Okay, that's pretty rough. But—" he said as JD reached for the tequila. "How's that better...or really different than mine? You pushed your girl away too, right? By fucking around and not getting your shit together in time?"

JD's eyes narrowed. "You really wanna do this?"

"Decide who's the biggest asshole at the table?" Carter asked. "Absolutely. Bring it."

"Okay." JD sat up a little straighter. "*Your* girl wants to be with you. All you have to do is go get her."

Carter leaned in and punched the table with his index finger with each word. "I'm. Not. Good. Enough. For. Her."

"So get good enough." JD shrugged as if that was no big deal.

"It's not that easy."

JD gave a humorless laugh. "Man, the good stuff isn't supposed to be easy."

Carter opened his mouth. Then snapped it shut. "Okay, so why don't you just go get your girl?"

"She's with someone else."

Carter frowned. "Mine was with someone else. And I hung back. Thought that was best."

"And?"

"Loved her so much it all hurt anyway. Just as much as if I'd gone in there from the start and fucked it up then."

JD nodded. "That sucks. But they must have broken up, huh?"

"Well, yeah. He died so…"

JD's eyes widened. "Damn."

"Yeah."

They sat for a long moment. Then JD said, "How'd it happen?"

"He was a cop. Got shot on the job."

"Fuck."

Again a long moment passed. Then JD said, "My girl got herself a surgeon. I don't think I can count on him dying to get her back."

They both, very inappropriately, snorted at that.

Then Carter handed the shot glasses over.

JD swigged both down and then chased the tequila with a gulp of beer.

"So what *are* you going to do to get her back?" Carter asked. "Because you have to at least try."

As he said the words out loud, they hit him hard in the chest. As if someone else was giving him the advice. Fuck.

"I don't know man. What can I do?"

Carter knew. And he couldn't believe he was going to say this, but…

"Whatever it takes. You have to at least make sure she *knows*, without a doubt, that you are crazy about her. That you love her. That she's the *one*. You might even have to go a little over the top."

If JD could land somewhere between Carter and his father, he'd probably be right on.

"Just—" he said before JD could respond. "Don't steal her dog or anything like that."

JD was studying him. "Whatever it takes, huh?"

Carter sighed. He couldn't believe he was advising someone to be more like Matt Shaw but, here they were. "Even if she chooses the other guy, don't let her do it *not* knowing how you feel."

JD nodded thoughtfully. "What about you?"

That was a good question. "I still need to figure some things out," Carter told him.

"Carter," JD said. "I can actually give *you* advice about that."

"Good. Lay it on me."

"Stop. Stop thinking. Stop worrying. Stop anything and everything that's keeping you away from her. If she loves you, she'll let you work on your stuff *with* her."

That sounded…right. Lacey would do that.

"Your girl didn't. She told you to get your shit together and *then* come find her," Carter pointed out.

"Because I wasn't even trying then," JD said. He scrubbed a hand over his face. "And then I never told her when I was trying. I thought I could do it on my own and then go to her, all new and right and ready. Don't do it my way."

Carter pulled in a long breath.

At least your dad tries. That was what Lacey had said. *He knows they might leave. But he keeps going after what he wants.*

Carter had always wondered how his dad kept getting women to fall in love with him even when he was so, so bad at relationships.

Maybe the trying just really mattered. Maybe there were enough people out there willing to give someone a chance if they were sincerely *trying.*

He hoped he could remember all of this in the morning.

"Carter."

Carter looked up to find Nolan standing next to the table. Nolan. The guy who was supposed to fix everything. It was kismet. Or some shit. "Nolan! Let me buy you a beer."

Nolan looked at the shot glasses and bottles and pitcher on the table. "I'm good, thanks."

"No, man, I'm not trying to get you into bed, I swear. This isn't about Lacey. Just beer."

"Uh, good to know. I'm actually here to give you a ride. In my car," he added quickly. "With me driving and you—" He sighed. "Jesus, everything sounds sexual now."

Carter tipped his head back and laughed again.

"Uh, hey guys." Michael LeClaire greeted them.

"Mikey! What are you doin' here?" JD asked with a big grin.

"Don't ever call me that," LeClaire said. "And Bailey called me."

Carter looked up at Nolan. "I didn't tell Bailey to call *you*."

"She's just a smart cookie I guess," Nolan said. "Come on, let's go."

Carter got unsteadily to his feet. He kind of wanted to be a belligerent pain in the ass like so many of the drunks he dealt with while on duty. It could be fun to be difficult and have such a great excuse. But in the end he knew he wouldn't do it. Drunks were the worst.

"I'm going to put my arm around you to help you walk to the door," Nolan said. "It's not an invitation."

"You're hilarious," Carter told him, wrapping an arm around Nolan's neck. "But I *will* tell you that I'm drunk enough that if you're going to cop a feel, now would be the time."

"You wish," Nolan muttered good-naturedly as they headed for the door.

The next thing Carter knew, he was waking up in his own bed, stripped to his boxers, with a jackhammer in his skull.

Dammit. He hated being hungover.

He dragged his ass out of bed, pulled on some sweatpants and headed downstairs.

The sound of snoring met him before he stepped into the living room.

Nolan was asleep in the recliner, his glasses crooked, his feet sticking out from the bottom of the blanket, snoring away.

But while Nolan was obviously a good friend and Carter appreciated that he'd had gotten him home so he didn't end up dead in a ditch, that was definitely not what took hold of Carter's heart and squeezed.

Lacey was there too.

She was asleep on the couch. She looked adorable, her hand tucked under her cheek, her hair falling over her face.

Lacey.

She was here.

"This is not exactly the threesome I had envisioned."

They both started awake. Lacey rolled and almost fell off the couch, Nolan's glasses fell onto his chest as he sat up quickly.

Carter moved past them into the kitchen. He really didn't want to deal with anything big or heavy or important right now.

His brain was pounding on the inside of his skull, punishing him for trying to drown it in tequila and beer, his stomach was roiling—and that was before the knot of tension had developed when he'd seen Lacey.

He didn't want to talk. He didn't want to listen. He didn't want to apologize or grovel or make any promises.

He wanted to drink coffee and feel sorry for himself.

He'd work on the apologies and promises and groveling tomorrow.

"Are you okay?" Lacey came into the kitchen but hovered in the doorway.

"No." He didn't look at her, just concentrated on pulling the coffee filters and grounds out of the cupboard.

He heard a thud behind him and turned to the back door. Mooch was butting his head against the glass.

Carter shook his head. That damned cat. Sure, Carter fed him. And let him sleep pretty much anywhere he wanted to in the house. And cleaned his litter box. And petted him some-times. But the cat wasn't his. He hadn't put a collar on it, he didn't hold it or let it sleep on his bed. Mooch was just a cat. He wasn't *Carter's* cat.

But every day when he heard the thud of Mooch's head against the back door, he smiled.

The cat kept coming back, even though Carter didn't really claim him.

Carter crossed to the door and opened it for the tabby. Mooch strolled in, rubbed against Carter's calf and then looked up with big golden eyes.

He knew what was going to happen. He knew that Carter was going to feed him and pet him and talk to him. Mooch trusted him and kept coming back, even though Carter kept him at arm's length. And strangely, the idea that Mooch trusted him anyway, made Carter all the more determined to be there and keep the cat food stocked and the litter box clean.

Suddenly Carter couldn't take a full breath.

Almost without thinking, Carter bent down and scooped the cat up.

He'd never held Mooch. Never picked him up before. But the cat didn't act alarmed in the slightest.

In fact, he rubbed his face against Carter's and started purring.

Carter felt his throat tighten.

Do not cry. For fuck's sake, do not cry over a stray cat purring for you. Jesus.

But it was touch-and-go for a minute.

Tequila was not his friend.

He ran his hand over Mooch's back, rubbed between his ears, and scratched under his chin. The cat's reaction was the very definition of bliss. The purring grew louder, he tucked his head against Carter's neck and his front paws began kneading Carter's chest.

The cat had been coming back for months, no matter what

Carter did or didn't do, and Carter realized that he had been resisting getting more attached. Mooch had just showed up one day out of the blue. Carter didn't know how long he would stay. Someday he could just not show up at the back door and that would be it. It would be over.

He pulled himself together, but kept hold of the cat, and turned to face Lacey. "What are you doing here?"

She lifted an eyebrow. "Making sure you're okay."

"I'm fine."

"You're not fine, Carter."

"I'm fine enough." He put Mooch down and filled the food and water dishes. The cat rubbed against him one more time and then buried his face in the food bowl.

"Carter—"

"I'm gonna go downtown for some coffee." He had a shift today too. That was going to be fun. But it was better than digging into all of this with Lacey. She'd ruined him for other women. He had to be the man she needed and deserved. He had to get over Garrett. He had to stop looking for other men to step in and fill that gap.

And if his fucking head would stop pounding for two minutes and his stomach would quit threatening to hurl its contents all over, he might be able to think about a couple of those things. Maybe.

But that wasn't going to happen anytime soon. Coffee was his best bet.

Oh, and avoiding all of this.

Lacey said nothing as he stalked past her on his way upstairs.

"What's—"

But Carter didn't stop to talk to Nolan.

He was going to have to thank the man for getting him home in one piece. But that would also have to wait. Nolan would want to turn it into some deep talk, no doubt, and that would definitely make Carter puke.

He knew what he needed to do. He just wasn't sure he could.

He needed to say goodbye to Garrett. For good. Finally.

And the pain in his chest at that thought was worse than the tequila-induced headache by ten.

Carter threw on some clothes, grabbed his wallet and keys and headed for the door.

"Carter."

Lacey's voice stopped him. Even as he knew he shouldn't. But he didn't turn to face her.

"I love you."

He gripped the doorknob tightly and pulled in a deep breath. She did. Somehow he knew that. Even though he didn't deserve it. And that was what drove him through the door and out to his truck.

He needed to start fucking deserving it.

CHAPTER
TWELVE

HE DROVE OUT OF TOWN, headed east, then turned onto the paved road that led to the cemetery.

When he got there, he slowed, but didn't make the turn in.

Garrett wasn't here. He'd been buried in Baton Rouge where his family was, where his life had been. Carter knew that his parents had talked about burying him here in Bad, in his hometown, where he'd spent so much of his life. But in the end, they'd bought a plot in Baton Rouge where other fallen policemen and women were buried and where they could visit and attend memorial services.

But Carter didn't need Garrett's plot to be here to visit with him and remember him.

Instead of taking the turn, Carter hit the accelerator and kept going. He drove six more miles down the road and then took the left that he'd taken so many times in his life. The dirt road led to Cooper's Hill, the party and make-out spot in high school. They'd drank and cussed and smoked and partied in that spot. They'd also watched the stars and talked about life and dreamed.

If Garrett's spirit was anywhere in Bad, it would be at Cooper's Hill.

Carter pulled up under one of the trees and turned the truck off. He sat staring out the windshield for almost five minutes before he got out.

He pushed himself up onto the hood and looked out over the fields that rolled slowly to the bayou. He'd seen this view a few hundred times in his life.

And he made himself think about Garrett. Not the good times, not the laughter, not the love—brotherly and otherwise. He made himself think about the fact that Garrett had been shot, had bled out and died in an alley in Baton Rouge, and was not coming back.

Carter felt a chill go through him and his mind start to block all of that, but he forced himself to stay on it, to really think about the fact that Garrett was gone. Forever.

He hadn't done that. At the funeral, he'd been face-to-face with Lacey and how much he loved her and the fact that he'd lost *her* and he'd been able to relegate losing Garrett to a corner of his mind where he didn't have to deal with it. He'd been sad. He'd let that much in. But he'd ignored the pain. Or maybe it was that the pain had blended into what he'd already been feeling being apart from Garrett and Lacey, being away from Baton Rouge, trying to start his life over in Bad and trying to get over the love that he hadn't been able to accept.

All of that hurt and confusion and frustration had felt so much like grief that the new sadness over Garrett hadn't really registered.

Now he made himself feel it.

The chill intensified, the pain in his chest grew, his mind repeating over and over *he's gone*.

Garrett was gone. There was no going back. There was no taking back words or redoing actions.

"I'm so sorry, man." He was surprised to hear his own voice out loud. But after a moment, he went on. "I'm so fucking sorry, Garrett. I never should have walked away. I should have talked to you about it. I should have told you more about how I felt.

But I know you loved her and…I'm very thankful that you shared her with me as much as you did."

She's still here.

The thought whispered through his mind and he was able to pull in a full breath.

"I miss you, man. I miss you so damned much."

Lacey's still here. You can still have the life full of love.

He breathed again, letting the remorse sink in. But then, surprisingly, he felt lighter.

He straightened and looked out over the rolling field of brown and green. He felt a breeze brush over his face.

Lacey was still here.

He let that thought really register. If *he* had been the one to die, he would have wanted to know that Garrett was there for her, loving her, giving her the happiness and the life she deserved.

Garrett was gone. Carter couldn't go back. But he could love her enough for him and Garrett. And she could love Carter enough for both of them too.

"I'll take care of her," he said. "I promise you, man, I'll take care of her. I can't replace you but I will do my best to make her laugh and be romantic and shower her with gifts and make sure she knows every day that she's loved."

Another breeze, stronger now, blew over his face, and Carter smiled.

"I'll even tell her your stupid jokes and I'll borrow your Batman costume for Halloween."

Carter felt his smile grow, thinking of all the things that had made Garrett Garrett. He could laugh at himself. He always wanted to be sure everyone around him was happy and he loved to give gifts for no reason. He said *I love you* easily, he made a big deal of holidays, and he never forgot a birthday. He was funny, inappropriately so at times, and was very into public displays of affection.

And, most of all, he didn't let the fear of things not lasting hold him back from doing all of that. From acting like a joyous, goofball. From making other people feel special, even those who might come and go from his life, who might even hurt him and break his heart.

Neither did Matt.

Carter's dad didn't do relationships right, and there was plenty there for him to work on, but Matt didn't let his mistakes keep him from loving people.

Carter needed to stop being afraid of messing up. Stop anything and everything that was keeping him away from Lacey, just like JD had said. *If she loves you, she'll let you work on your stuff with her.* That, above all else, was who Lacey was. She would love him through his screw-ups.

As Carter thought about all of the ways Garrett had made people smile and laugh and feel special, he felt the tightness in his chest loosen. He could be more like that. He *should be* more like that. He needed to stop being half of the guy Lacey needed and work on being *the* guy. Because he was the only one left. No one else in the world would love her like he would.

Trying to be more like Garrett in the process would only make him a better man.

With one last look over the valley and a deep breath, Carter slid to the ground and got back in the truck. He had a shift to do and then he and Lacey needed to talk.

With roses. And candles. And maybe some chocolate cheesecake.

He pulled into the convenience store on the end of Main Street. He knew they wouldn't have chocolate cheesecake but maybe he could make due with cookies or something for one night. Lacey would appreciate the thought. She knew that he didn't do dessert by candlelight. She'd understand the gesture.

He was debating between chocolate chip and peanut butter when the bell over the door jingled as someone came into the store. He glanced over. And froze.

It was Lacey.

In a trench coat.

She walked straight to him. "We need to talk."

He looked down at the cookies. Dammit. He really wanted to make this gesture. It would mean more than just a bunch of words. He needed to *show* her that he was changing. He wanted to. Now that he had the surprise in mind, he really wanted a chance to pull it off.

"Yes, we do," he agreed. "Later."

"Now. I'm done waiting."

Dammit. Just when he was getting romantic…

"Lacey, seriously, later we'll go over everything. I promise that—"

"Now, Carter."

He frowned. "Later."

"I want to—"

"Lacey," he cut in. "I need to get to work. I don't have time for this. We'll talk *later*."

When she saw the candles she'd feel bad about not trusting him on this.

She hesitated—then she looked around, grabbed three candy bars off the shelf, tucked them into the pocket of the trench coat and headed for the door.

"What are you doing?"

She looked at him over her shoulder. "Giving you some work to do." Then she pushed the door open and walked outside.

She'd just shoplifted three candy bars.

Carter sighed. He glanced over at the shop owner. "You want to press charges, Steve?"

Steve looked from Lacey's back out the window to Carter. He looked amused. "Yeah, I think I do."

Carter sighed again. Great.

He started after Lacey. She had just gotten into her car.

He strode toward her and knocked on the window. When she looked up, he motioned with his hand for her to roll it down.

"Is there a problem, officer?"

He put his hands on his hips. "Ms. Andrews, I'm going to have to ask you to return to the store."

She looked at the storefront. "I don't think so."

"If you refuse, I'll have to take you downtown to the station."

She shrugged. "Well, you gotta do what you gotta do."

"Lacey, I get it. You want to talk. But this is crazy."

She started the car.

"You can't leave."

"Of course I can."

"I'll have to pursue you."

"I can't think of anything I'd like more."

Her words shut him up for a moment. He moved in closer to the window. "If you want me to use my handcuffs, all you have to do is ask, Lace."

She gave him an impish grin. "I do. Very much." Then she shifted into reverse and started to inch backward.

"Lacey!"

"Stop me and take me to the station or let me go. Those are your choices."

"Or you could return the candy bars and we'll call it a momentary lapse in judgement."

"Can we talk for a few minutes?"

"*Later.*"

"I'm not returning the candy bars."

Oh for fuck's sake. He turned and stomped to his truck, jerked the glove compartment open, removed his handcuffs and stomped back to her car.

"Get out of the car, Ms. Andrews."

She did.

"You have the right to remain silent." He read her the rest of the rights as he escorted her to his truck. It wasn't his squad car but he put her in back of the extended cab anyway. They didn't speak on the way to the station.

Once inside, he took her to a holding cell. "This what you want?"

"You don't need to question me in one of those rooms like on TV?" she asked.

"I witnessed your crime. I don't have any questions."

"I have a few things I'd like to say. On the record," she told him.

"Fine. *Later.*" He resisted smirking until he'd turned away from her.

He might be adopting a few of Garrett's traits and habits, but he wasn't changing completely. And Carter Shaw liked to get his way.

"Do I get a phone call?"

"Oh sure." That meant Nolan would be down here in a few minutes. He turned and hollered for Marie, the front desk clerk. "Will you bring Ms. Andrews the phone?"

Marie looked completely indifferent but she brought the station's cordless phone.

"I'll be back," he said, starting down the hall.

"When?" she asked

"Later."

He was grinning as he headed for his desk.

———

He was not grinning fifteen minutes later when he was confronted with Lacey's one phone call.

Coach Karr.

"Carter."

"Coach."

Dammit. How did Lacey have Coach's phone number?

"You're going to post bail for Lacey?" Carter asked.

There was no bail. She hadn't been formerly booked or even officially arrested. Steve wasn't going to press charges. The three candy bars came to four dollars and some odd change. Carter would give him ten and Dave would think it had all worked out great.

"She didn't ask for bail. Just for this." Coach held up a bottle of water and a sandwich.

"You're bringing her lunch?"

"That's what she asked for."

"She didn't ask for you to help her get out of here?"

"No. She doesn't want to leave."

Carter sighed. "Why is she acting crazy?"

"Because she loves you and is afraid of losing you."

Carter frowned. "I'm not going anywhere."

"Not physically maybe." Coach set the water and sandwich to the side and leaned in on the countertop. "That's why she came to Bad. She knew you weren't going anywhere. But emotionally, you're a flight risk."

Carter shook his head. "I'm crazy about her. Like *crazy*. Obsessed. I'm not the one at risk of leaving in any way."

Coach chuckled. "You're always the one leaving, boy. That's why you haven't been with anyone serious or long term."

"No, other people leave," Carter insisted. He had always been aware of this emotional issue. He'd always known that he avoided connections because he had formed them and had them broken so many times growing up.

"*You're* the one leaving," Coach repeated, pointing a finger at Carter's nose. "You left Bad as soon as you graduated, you left Baton Rouge as soon as things got serious there, and you left Lacey the other night."

Damn, Lacey had filled Coach in on a lot, apparently. But still Carter shook his head. "I went to college, then I moved back here to help my dad, and I made *her* leave the other night."

"Before she could hurt you by leaving herself."

Carter felt his heart thumping, the blood rushing through his body. "No."

"Yes. You left Bad after high school because your friends and classmates were leaving and you couldn't watch them go. You left Baton Rouge after Lacey was out of reach. You try to leave before people can leave you. You've been left a lot and you had to take control and keep your heart safe."

Carter felt his throat squeezing. Jesus. How did Coach know all of that?

"But for the past ten months, you've been unable to get past the hurt of Garrett's death because it isn't just that he's gone…he *left* you too."

Carter swallowed hard. "I left him first," he managed.

"Yes. And you've been regretting it ever since. You've been conflicted because Garrett was the first person who left who didn't want to and you've been beating yourself up for leaving him and missing out on those last two months you would have had together."

Carter nodded, unable to speak.

"So don't do that with Lacey."

"I can't," he choked out. "That's the problem. I *can't* leave her. I had to make her leave."

"She might have been the one to leave the house, but you were the one who left the situation emotionally."

Carter dropped his head to one of his hands, rubbing his forehead. "Because making her go when she didn't want to was easier than watching her go because she *did* want to."

"But she didn't go."

Coach's words were soft and simple.

Carter looked up at him. "What?"

"She never left Bad. She left your house, but she was here the whole time, waiting for you."

Carter straightened. "She never left town?"

"No. And that's something you need to start thinking about — there are a hell of a lot of people who *haven't* left. Lacey. *Me.* Your other friends. Even if they're not *here* physically all the time, they're here for you if you need them." Coach moved around the end of the counter and came to stand by Carter. He put his hand on Carter's shoulder. "And Garrett didn't want to leave you, Carter."

"I know," Carter said hoarsely.

"And your dad," Coach added. "He's never left you, son."

"He drove them away."

Coach shrugged. "That's not how I see it."

Carter frowned. "How do you see it?"

"Your dad was hurt by your mother. So with the other women, he pushed them, testing to see if they'd really stick by him. And none of them did."

"He shouldn't have to test them," Carter said. "If you love someone and they love you, you just know it. It shouldn't be a test."

Coach's face relaxed into a smile. "Exactly."

Carter started to ask what he was talking about, but just then Lacey came strolling up front from the holding cell.

"I'm starving," she announced.

And clearly she'd figured out that he hadn't really locked her in there.

"Hope peanut butter and jelly is okay," Coach said, handing her the sandwich and water he'd brought.

"My favorite," she said. Her eyes locked with Carter's. "I appreciate it, Coach. I might be here for a while."

Coach clapped Carter on the back. "Looks like my work is done here. I'll see you both later."

Carter watched his coach and mentor walk away. Just as Coach reached the door, Carter called, "Hey, Coach."

Coach Karr turned back. "Yeah?"

"Thanks for always being there."

He grinned. "No place I'd rather be."

The door bumped shut behind him and Carter turned to Lacey. He held up his handcuffs. "If you do what you're told, I'll use these on you."

She looked from the cuffs to his face and grinned. "I don't think that's how it goes."

"No?"

"I think I'm supposed to get handcuffed only if I'm *bad*."

"I'll show you bad." He bent and scooped her up and put her on the countertop.

"Carter!" But she was laughing.

He moved in between her knees, his hands on her hips and his eyes on hers. "I was going to do candles and roses and the whole bit but I can't wait another second. I love you, Lacey. Marry me."

She wrapped her arms around his neck. "Yes."

He laughed. "You don't need a bunch of promises and apologies and to know what changed my mind?"

"Sure. But not before I tell you that I love you and want to be with you forever and say yes to marrying you," she said.

He kissed her, long and sweet.

When he pulled back, he said, "I'm not going anywhere ever again."

She hugged him. "I know."

"And I'm sorry it took me so long to be the man you needed. The *whole* man. I'm in for all of it. I'm going to screw up, I'm sure, but I'll keep trying."

She blinked, her eyes sparkling with tears. "And when you screw up, you'll have your best friend there to talk you through it and help you figure out how to fix it."

Carter felt warmth spread through his chest and contentment wrap around him. She was right. Garrett was gone, but he still had a lot of amazing people in his life who would be here for him. Jackson. And Nolan. And JD. He and JD were definitely going to hang out some more.

He leaned in and kissed her again, pouring all of his love into it. She pressed close and when he lifted his head, she put her lips to his ear.

"By the way, you knocked your best friend up after all, so you might want to get that engagement ring sooner versus later."

He jerked back and stared at her.

"The first test was a dud I guess," she said. "The next three all had two lines."

That sunk in surprisingly fast. "I knew Nolan was going to take advantage of me when I was drunk."

Lacey laughed and hugged him tight. "Oh no, you're all mine. Only mine."

He pulled her close, wrapping her in a huge hug, and buried his face in her hair. She was his best friend, the love of his life, and soon to be his wife and mother of his child.

Garrett was no doubt grinning like an idiot wherever he was.

———

Thank you so much for reading Carter and Lacey's story! There's a lot more sexy, fun from Bad!

These books are all standalones and don't need to be read in any particular order!

The Best Bad Boy: (Jase and Priscilla)
A bad boy-good girl, small town romance

Bad Medicine: (Brooke and Nick)
A hot boss, medical, small town romance

Bad Influence: (Marc and Sabrina)
An enemies to lovers, road trip / stuck together, small town romance

Bad Taste in Men: (Luke and Bailey)
A friends to lovers, gettin'-her-groove back, small town romance

Not Such a Bad Guy: (Regan and Christopher)

A one-night-stand, mistaken identity, small town romance

Return of the Bad Boy: (Jackson and Annabelle)
A bad boy-good girl, fake relationship, small town romance

Bad Behavior: (Carter and Lacey)
A bad boy-good girl, second chance small town romance

Got It Bad: (Nolan and Randi)
A nerd-tomboy, opposites attract, small town romance

Find all of my books at
ErinNicholas.com

ⴲ
And join in on all the FAN FUN!

Join my **email list!**
bit.ly/Keep-In-Touch-Erin
(be sure you get those dashes and capital letters in there!)

And be the first to hear about my news, sales, freebies, behind-the-scenes, and more!

Or for even more fun, join my **Super Fan page** on Facebook and chat with me and other super fans every day! Just search Facebook for Erin Nicholas Super Fans!

WANT MORE FROM THE BAYOU?

There's so much more from Erin's Louisiana bayou world!

Head down the road to Autre next and dive into the Boys of the Bayou series (where you'll first meet the Landry family)!

All available now!

My Best Friend's Mardi Gras Wedding

Sweet Home Louisiana

Beauty and the Bayou

Crazy Rich Cajuns

Must Love Alligators

Four Weddings and a Swamp Boat Tour

———

And be sure to check out **the connected rom com series,**
Boys of the Bayou-Gone Wild

Otterly Irresistible

Heavy Petting

Flipping Love You

Sealed With A Kiss

Say It Like You Mane It

Head Over Hooves

Kiss My Giraffe

———

And the **Badges of the Bayou** (where you get to know Michael LeClaire and JD Evans!)

Gotta Be Bayou

Bayou With Benefits

Rocked Bayou

Stand Bayou

Stuck Bayou

Just Wanna Be Bayou

———

And MUCH more—

including my printable booklist— at

ErinNicholas.com

ABOUT ERIN

Erin Nicholas is the New York Times and USA Today bestselling author of over forty sexy contemporary romances. Her stories have been described as toe-curling, enchanting, steamy and fun. She loves to write about reluctant heroes, imperfect heroines and happily ever afters. She lives in the Midwest with her husband who only wants to read the sex scenes in her books, her kids who will never read the sex scenes in her books, and family and friends who say they're shocked by the sex scenes in her books (yeah, right!).

Find her and all her books at
www.ErinNicholas.com

And find her on Facebook, Goodreads, BookBub, and Instagram!